For Laurie Keller, the best friend I have never met,
who made me feel big and strong when I was
feeling small and scared. Thank you.

Text and illustrations copyright © 2017 JoAnn Adinolfi
Book design by Simon Stahl

No animals or snowflakes were harmed in the making of this book.

CIP data for this book is available from the Library of Congress.

Published by Creston Books, LLC
www.crestonbooks.co

FSC
www.fsc.org
MIX
Paper from
responsible sources
FSC® C002589

Type set in Chocolate Covered Raindrops by Vanessa Bays and Mighty Zeo by Blambot
Source of Production: Worzalla Books, Stevens Point, Wisconsin
Printed and bound in the United States of America
1 2 3 4 5

# The CHILLY ADVENTURES of Mr. Small

*A freezing story in words and pictures by*
**JoAnn Adinolfi**

Creston Books

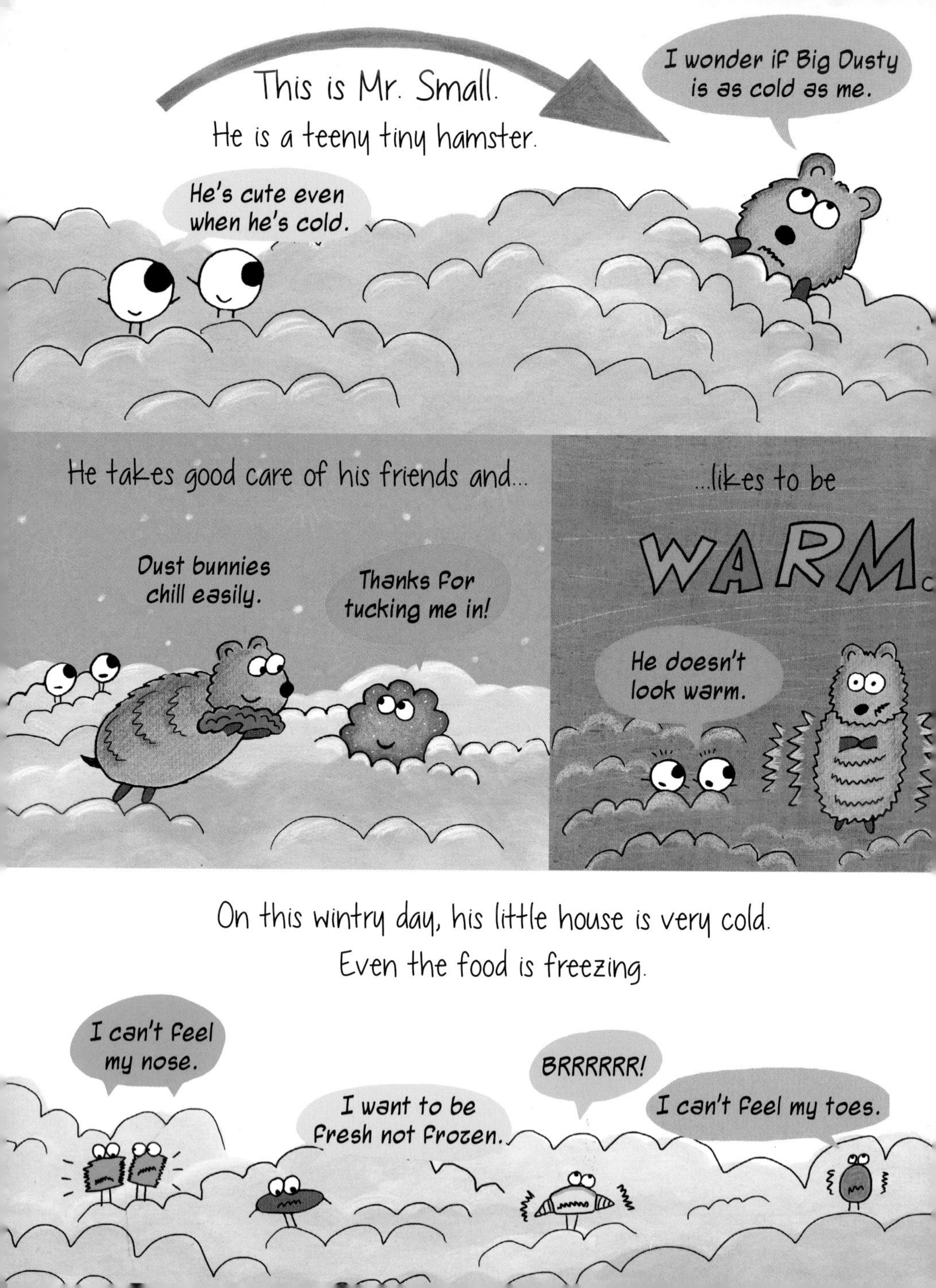
This is Mr. Small.
He is a teeny tiny hamster.
I wonder if Big Dusty is as cold as me.
He's cute even when he's cold.
He takes good care of his friends and...
Dust bunnies chill easily.
Thanks for tucking me in!
...likes to be
WARM.
He doesn't look warm.
On this wintry day, his little house is very cold.
Even the food is freezing.
I can't feel my nose.
I want to be fresh not frozen.
BRRRRRR!
I can't feel my toes.

Looks like he's got everything in his house except

# HEAT.

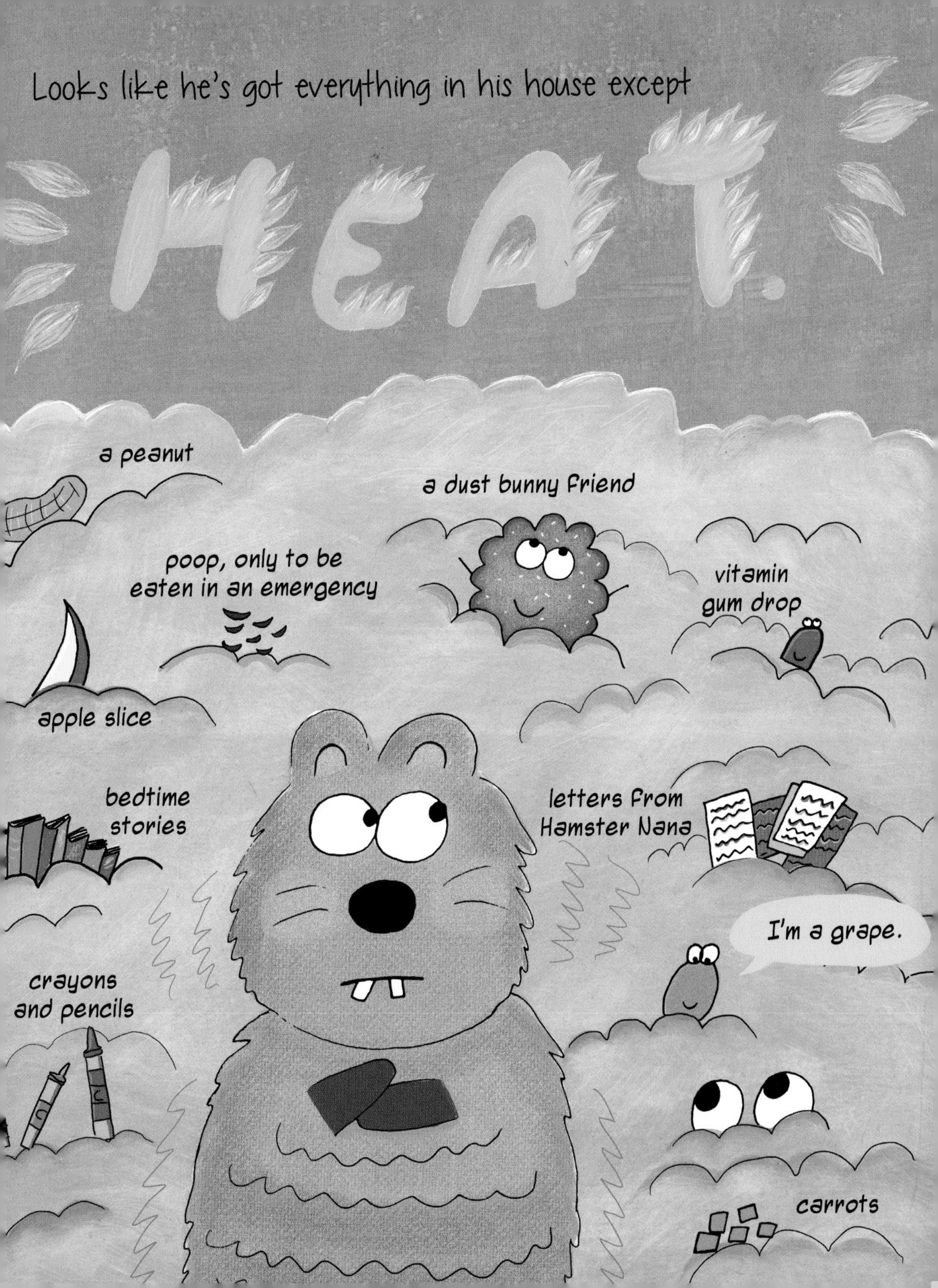
a peanut
a dust bunny friend
poop, only to be eaten in an emergency
vitamin gum drop
apple slice
bedtime stories
letters from Hamster Nana
I'm a grape.
crayons and pencils
carrots

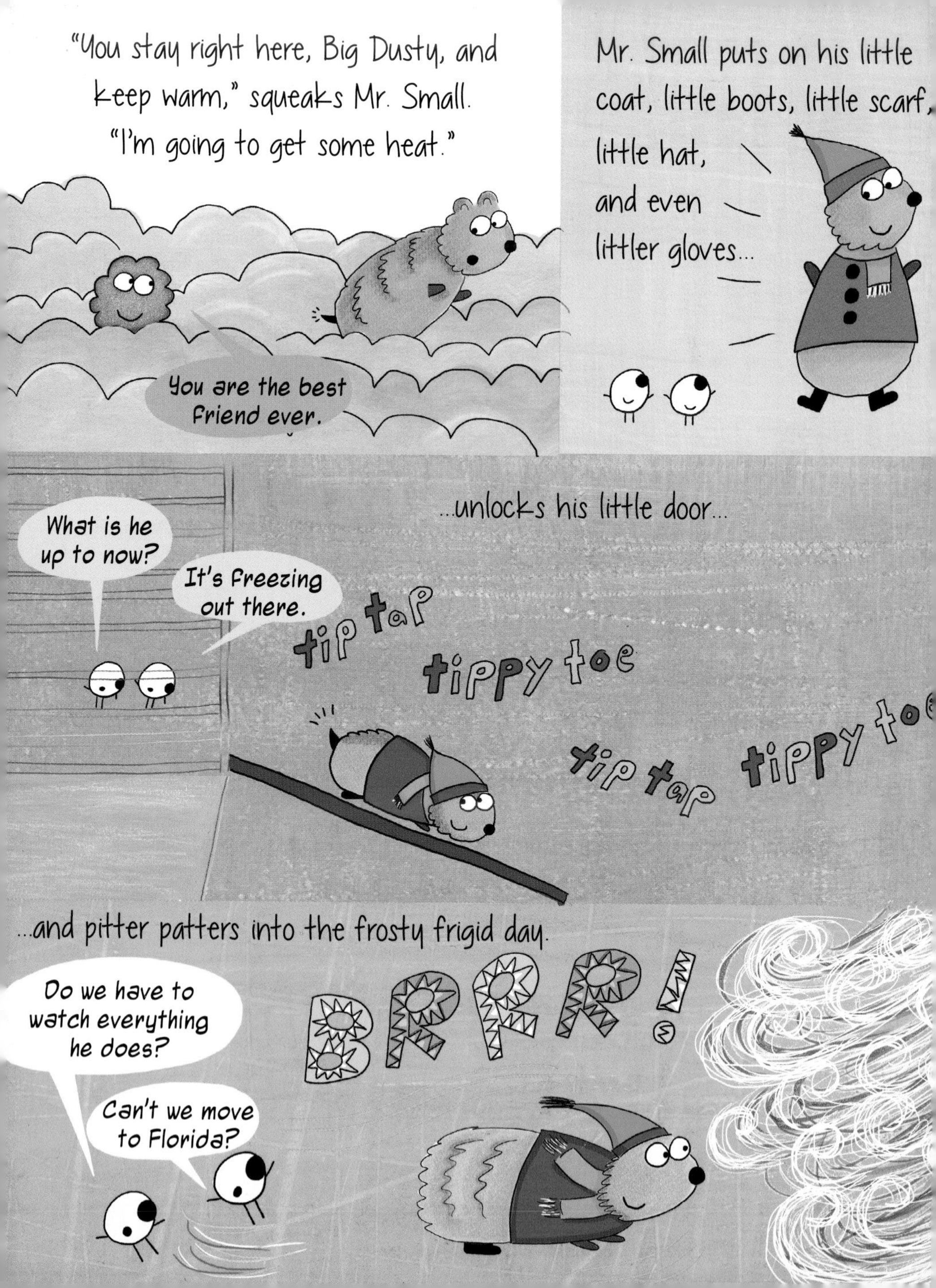
"You stay right here, Big Dusty, and keep warm," squeaks Mr. Small. "I'm going to get some heat."
You are the best friend ever.
Mr. Small puts on his little coat, little boots, little scarf, little hat, and even littler gloves...
...unlocks his little door...
What is he up to now?
It's freezing out there.
tip tap
tippy toe
tip tap
tippy toe
...and pitter patters into the frosty frigid day.
Do we have to watch everything he does?
Can't we move to Florida?
BRRR!

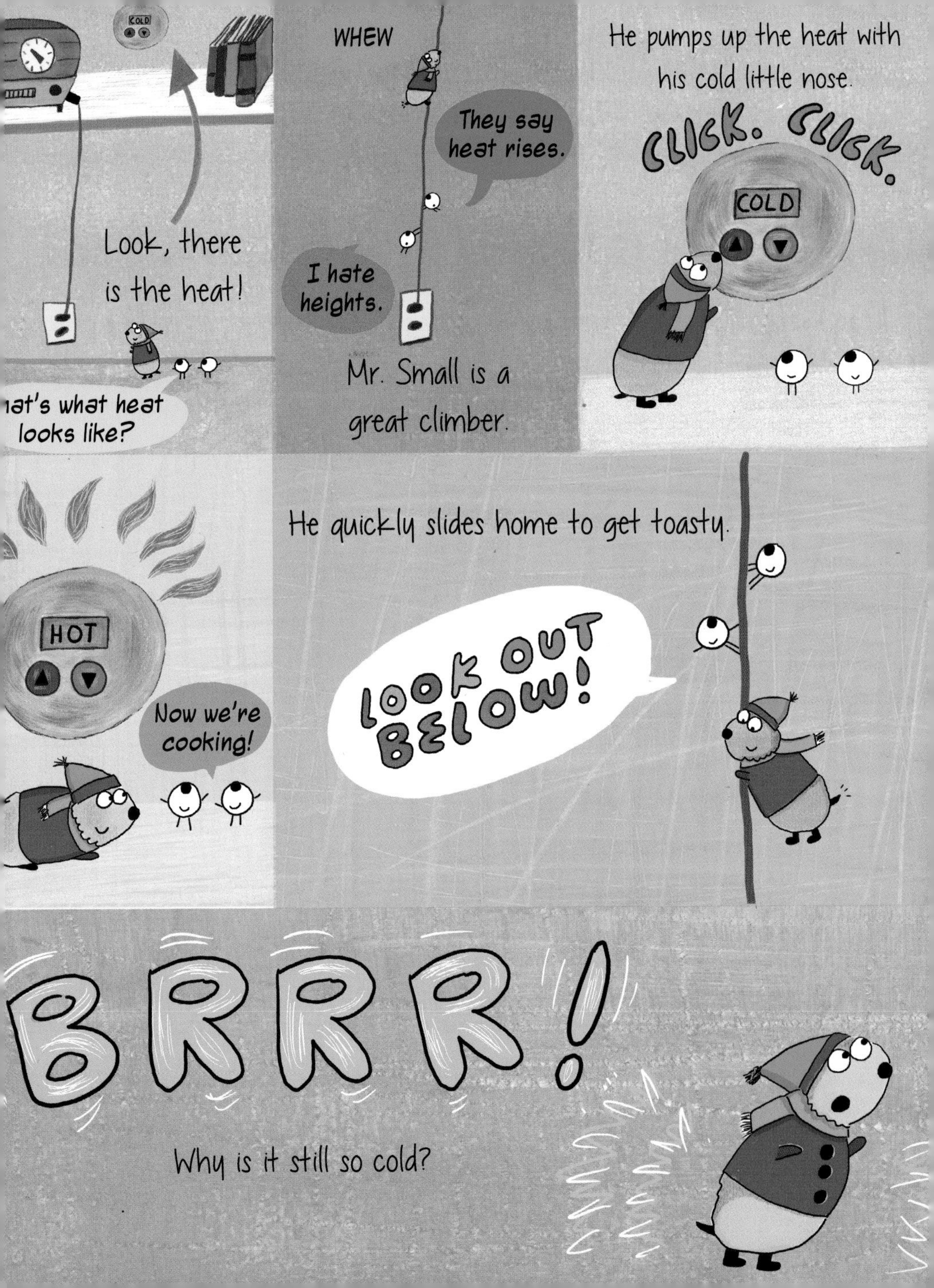
COLD
Look, there is the heat!
at's what heat looks like?
WHEW
They say heat rises.
I hate heights.
Mr. Small is a great climber.
He pumps up the heat with his cold little nose.
CLICK. CLICK.
COLD
HOT
Now we're cooking!
He quickly slides home to get toasty.
LOOK OUT BELOW!
BRRR!
Why is it still so cold?

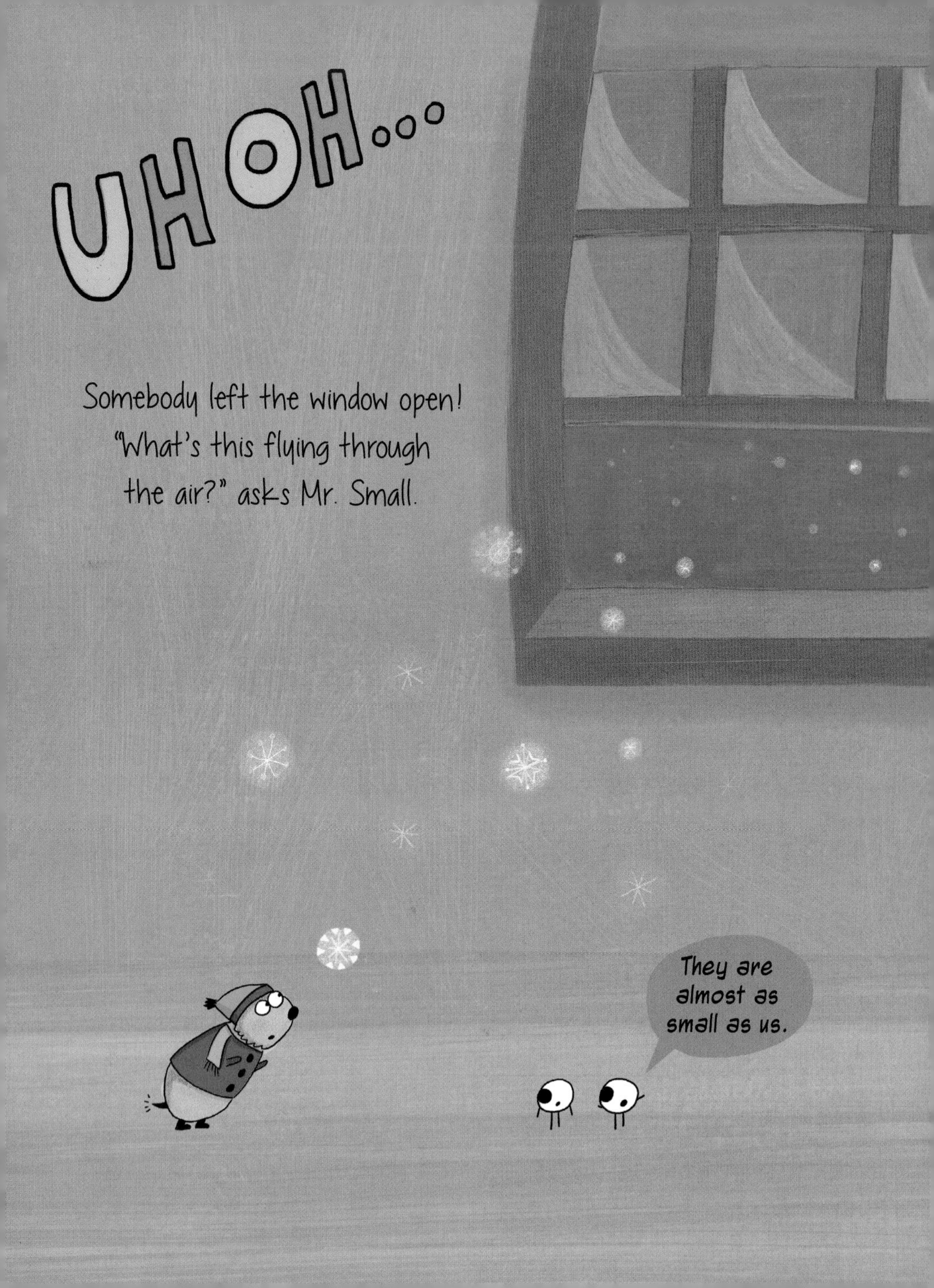
UH OH...
They are almost as small as us.

Somebody left the window open!
"What's this flying through the air?" asks Mr. Small.

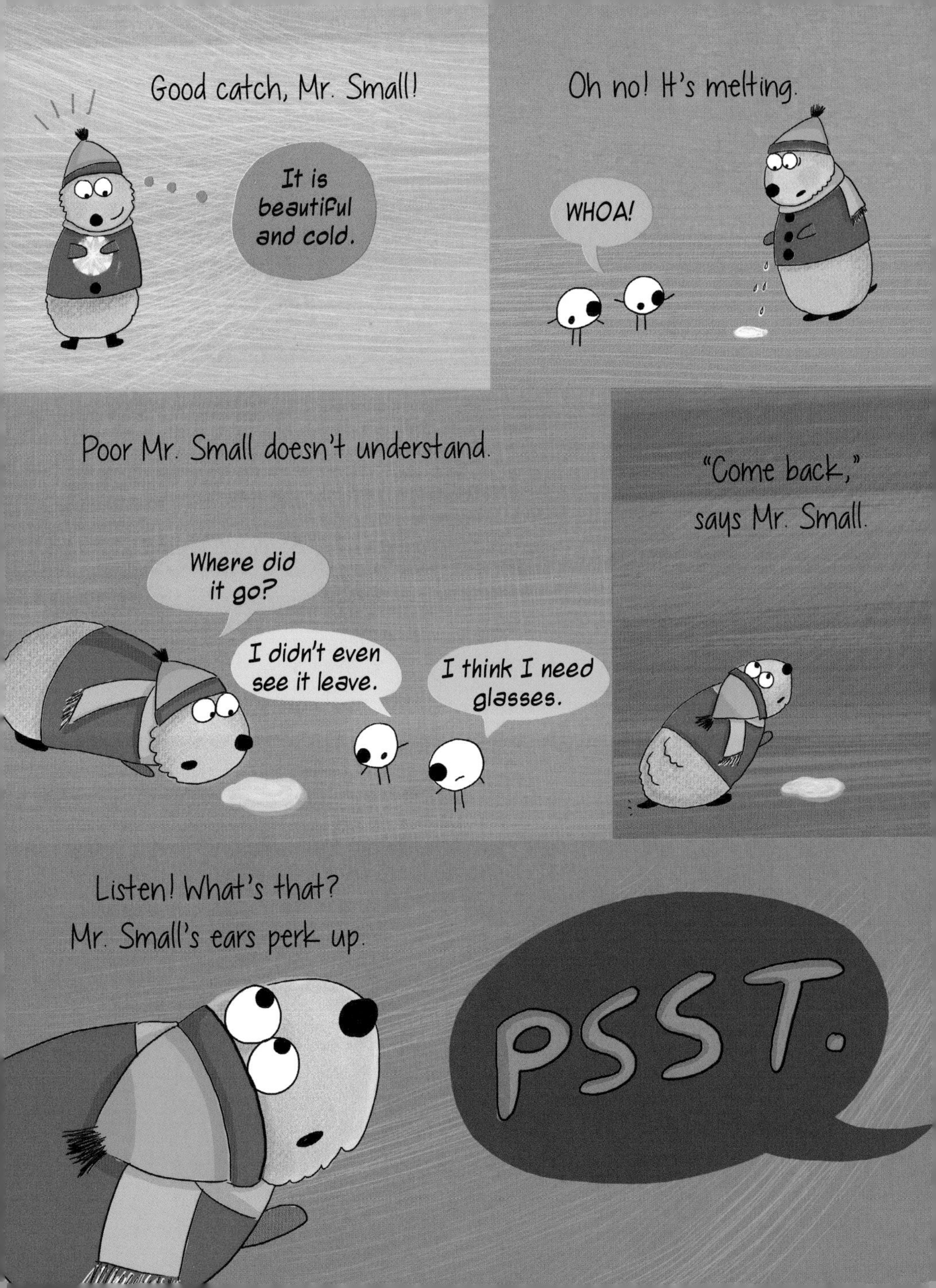
Good catch, Mr. Small!
It is beautiful and cold.
Oh no! It's melting.
WHOA!
Poor Mr. Small doesn't understand.
Where did it go?
I didn't even see it leave.
I think I need glasses.
"Come back," says Mr. Small.
Listen! What's that?
Mr. Small's ears perk up.
PSST.

Mr. Small can't believe his eyes. There is the little cold thing he had just been holding in his hands.

The strangers introduce themselves.

I am Chilly. I am a snowflake. What are you?

I am Mr. Small. I am a hamster.

Hi, we're googly eyes.

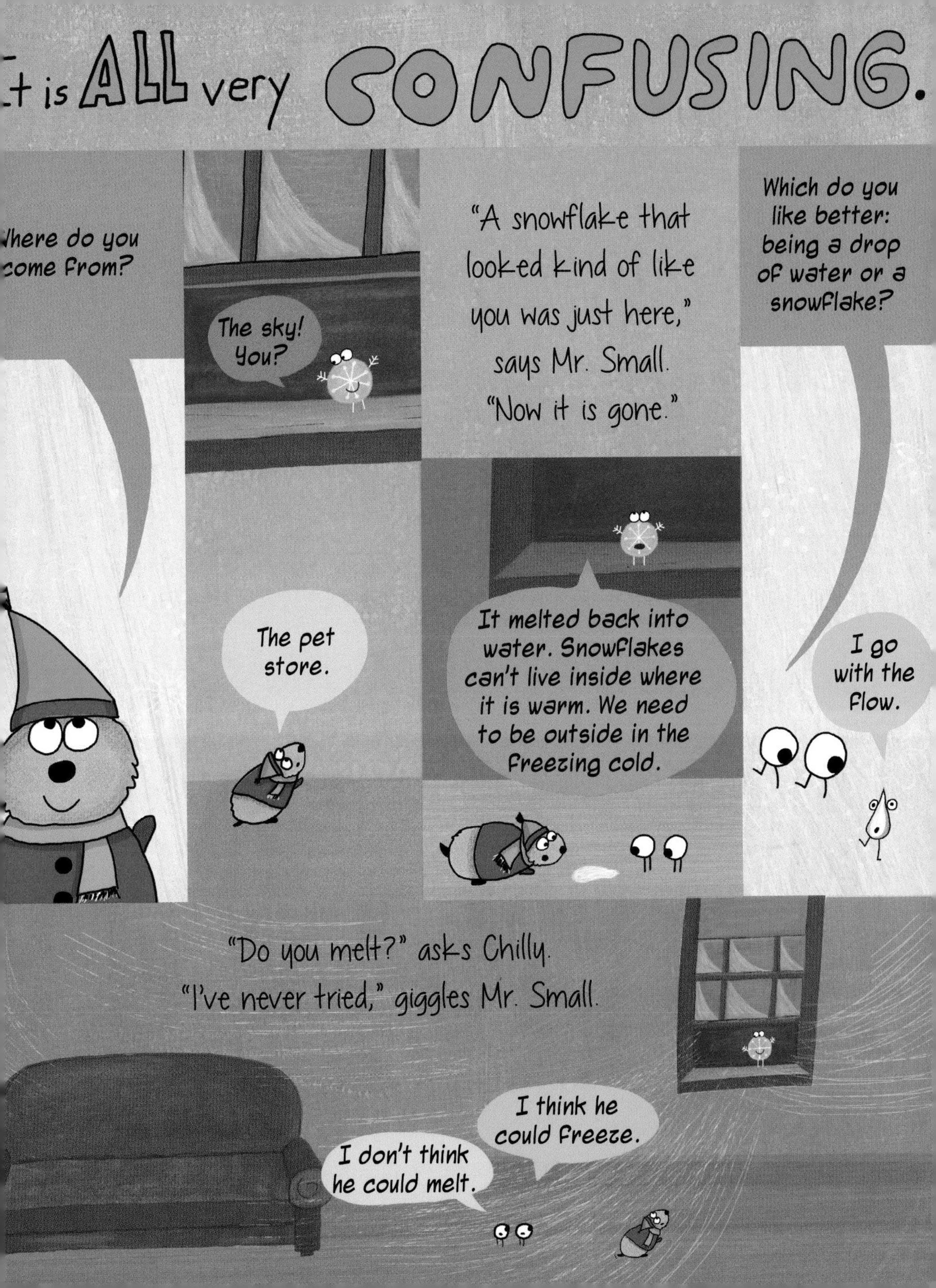
t is ALL very CONFUSING.
here do you
ome from?
The sky! You?
The pet store.
"A snowflake that looked kind of like you was just here," says Mr. Small. "Now it is gone."
It melted back into water. Snowflakes can't live inside where it is warm. We need to be outside in the freezing cold.
Which do you like better: being a drop of water or a snowflake?
I go with the flow.
"Do you melt?" asks Chilly.
"I've never tried," giggles Mr. Small.
I think he could freeze.
I don't think he could melt.

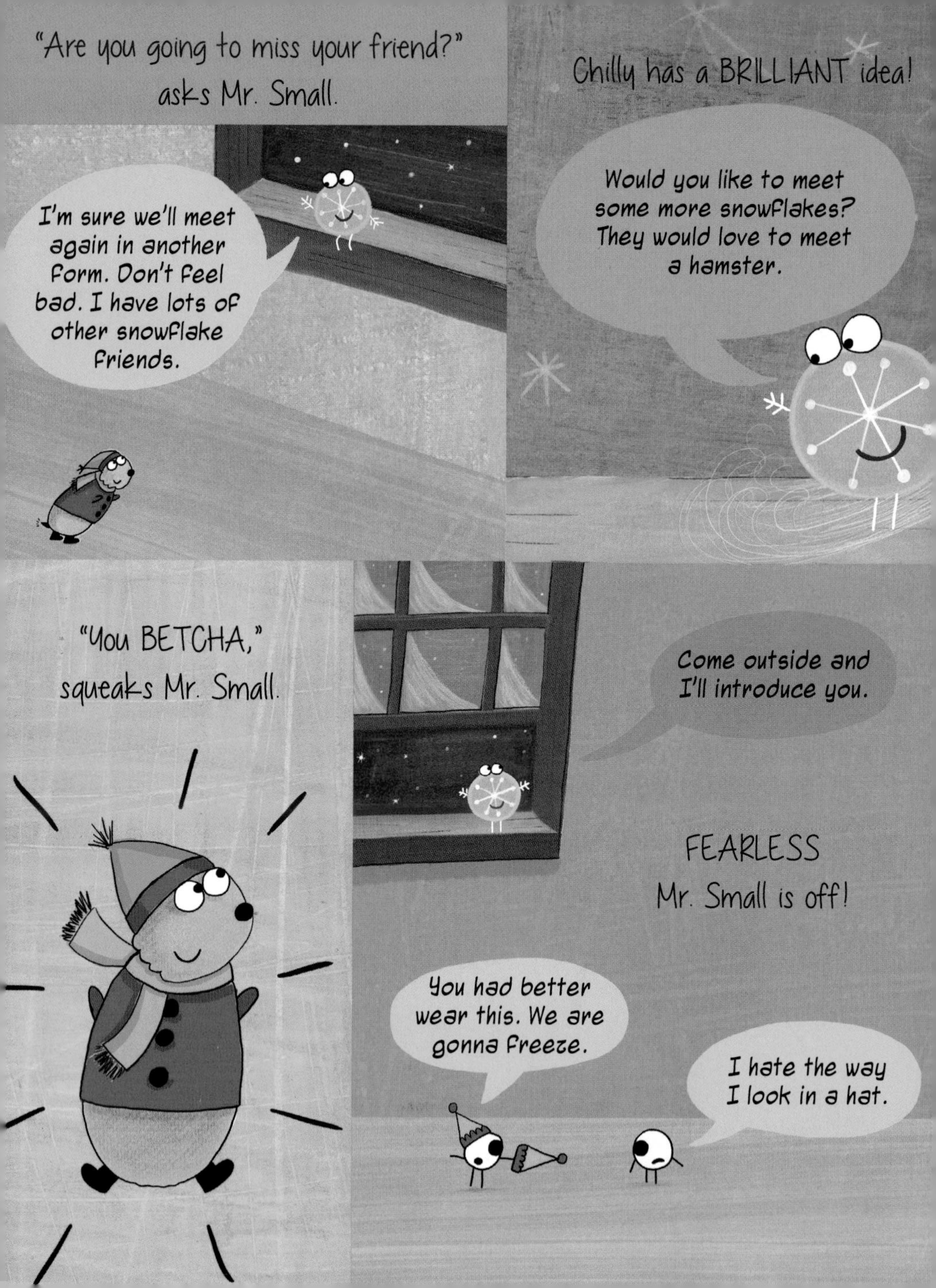
"Are you going to miss your friend?" asks Mr. Small.
I'm sure we'll meet again in another form. Don't feel bad. I have lots of other snowflake friends.
Chilly has a BRILLIANT idea!
Would you like to meet some more snowflakes? They would love to meet a hamster.
"You BETCHA," squeaks Mr. Small.
Come outside and I'll introduce you.
FEARLESS Mr. Small is off!
You had better wear this. We are gonna freeze.
I hate the way I look in a hat.

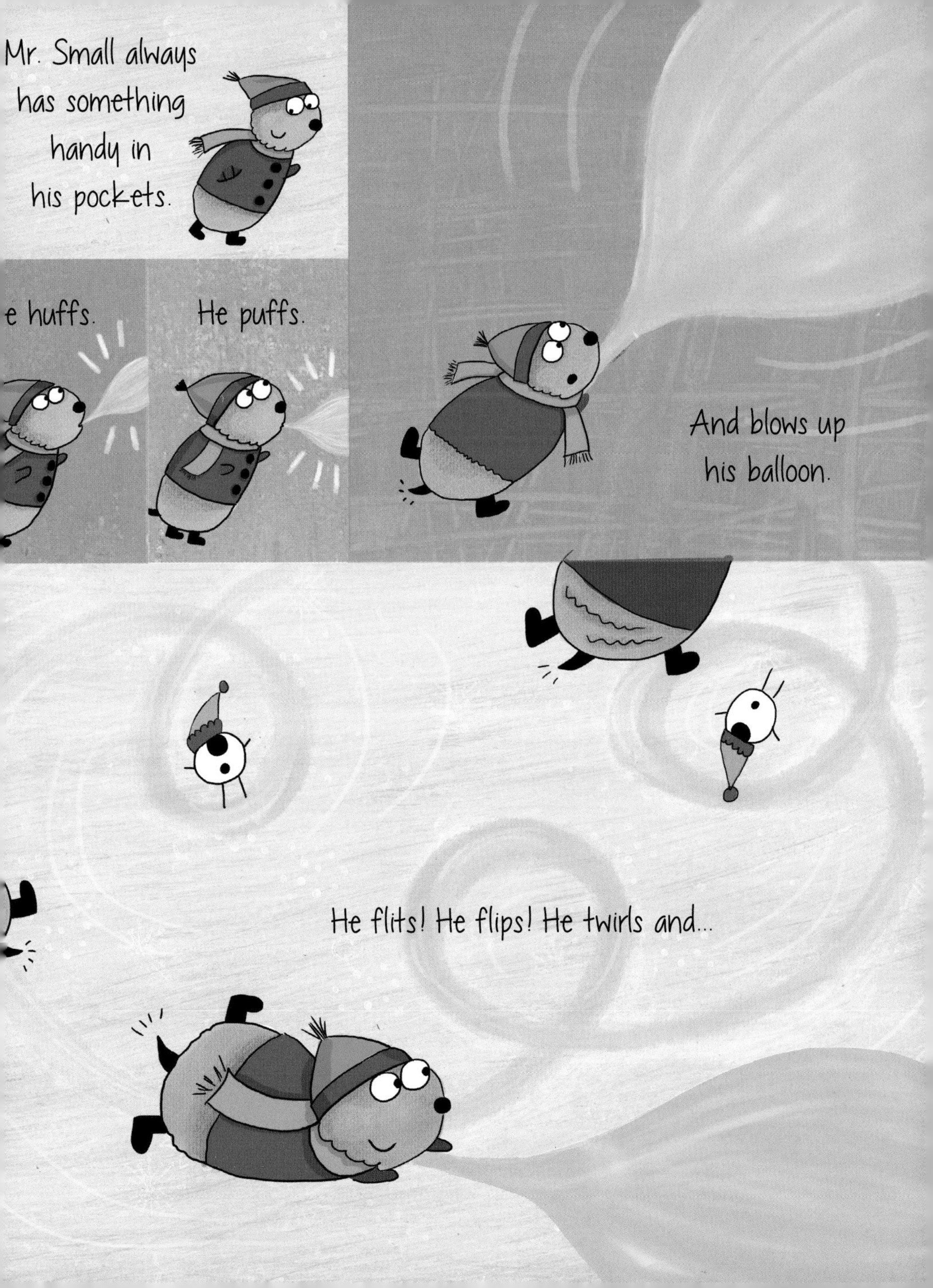
Mr. Small always has something handy in his pockets.
e huffs.
He puffs.
And blows up his balloon.
He flits! He flips! He twirls and...

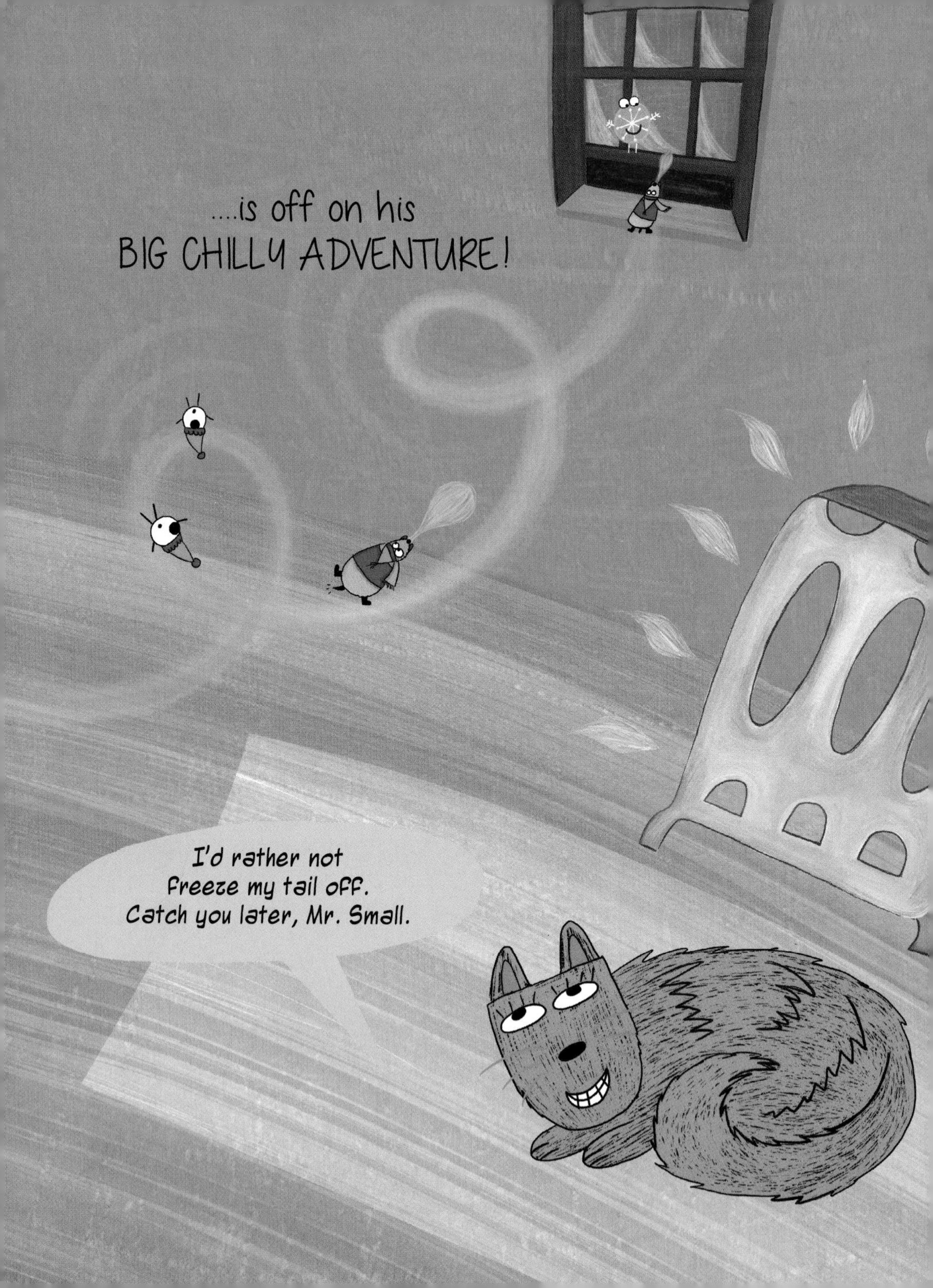
....is off on his
BIG CHILLY ADVENTURE!
I'd rather not freeze my tail off. Catch you later, Mr. Small.

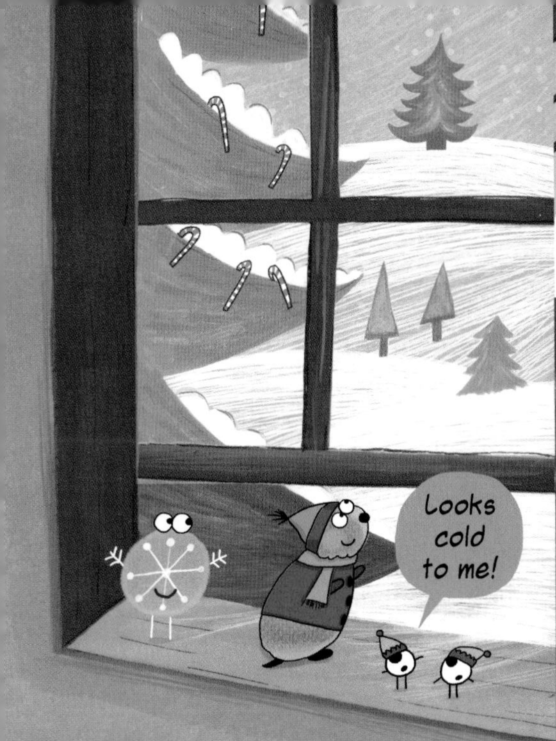
Looks cold to me!

"It doesn't look cold at all," says Mr. Small. "It looks warm and cozy like a big, white blanket."

Mr. Small leaps into the fluff. WHEE!

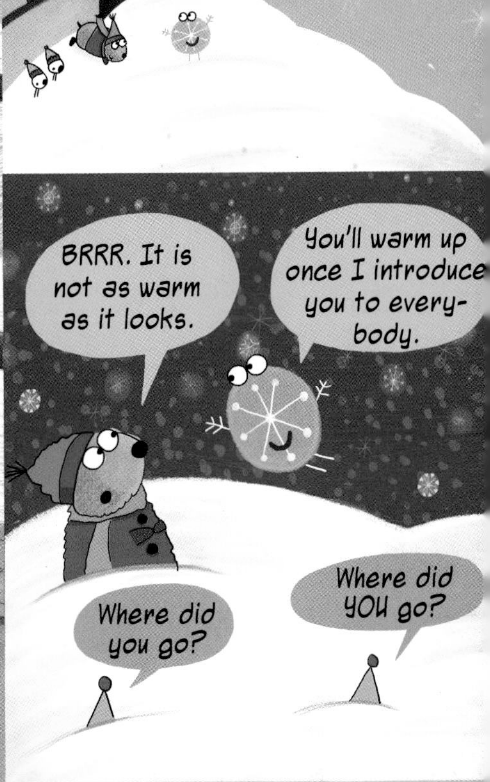
BRRR. It is not as warm as it looks.
You'll warm up once I introduce you to every-body.
Where did you go?
Where did YOU go?

"Hey everybody," says Chilly. "This is Mr. Small. Mr. Small, say hi to: Crystal, Ice, Nippy, Brisk, and Crisp."

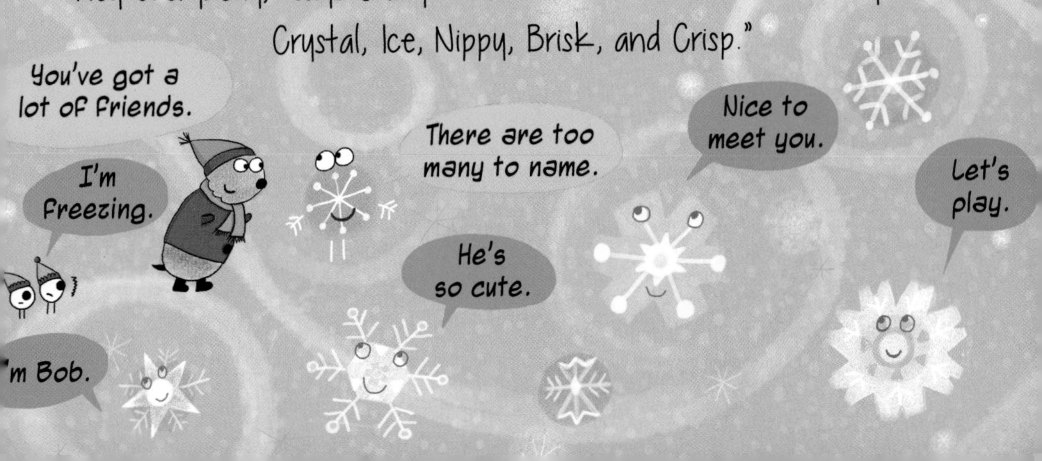
You've got a lot of friends.
I'm freezing.
There are too many to name.
Nice to meet you.
Let's play.
He's so cute.
'm Bob.

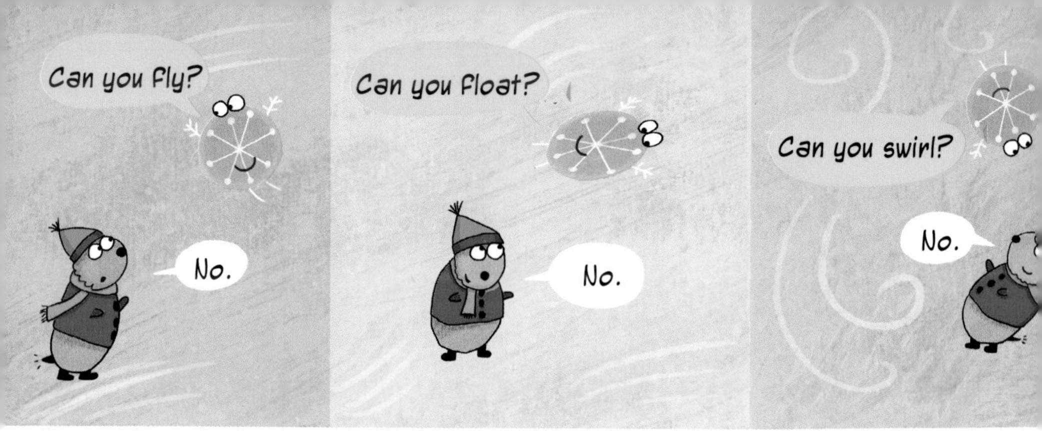
Can you fly?
No.
Can you float?
No.
Can you swirl?
No.

"Mmm," says Chilly.
"I guess we'll have to ski.
Stick these on."

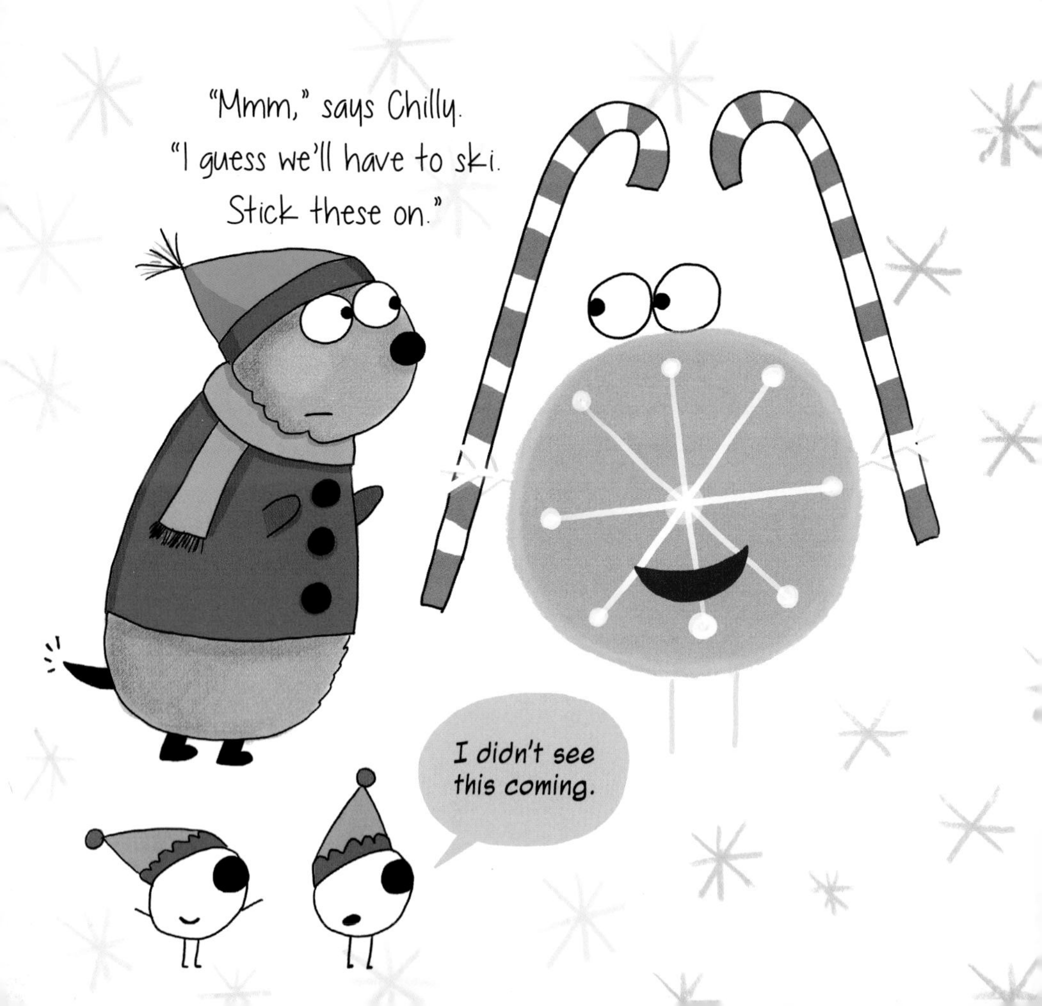
I didn't see this coming.

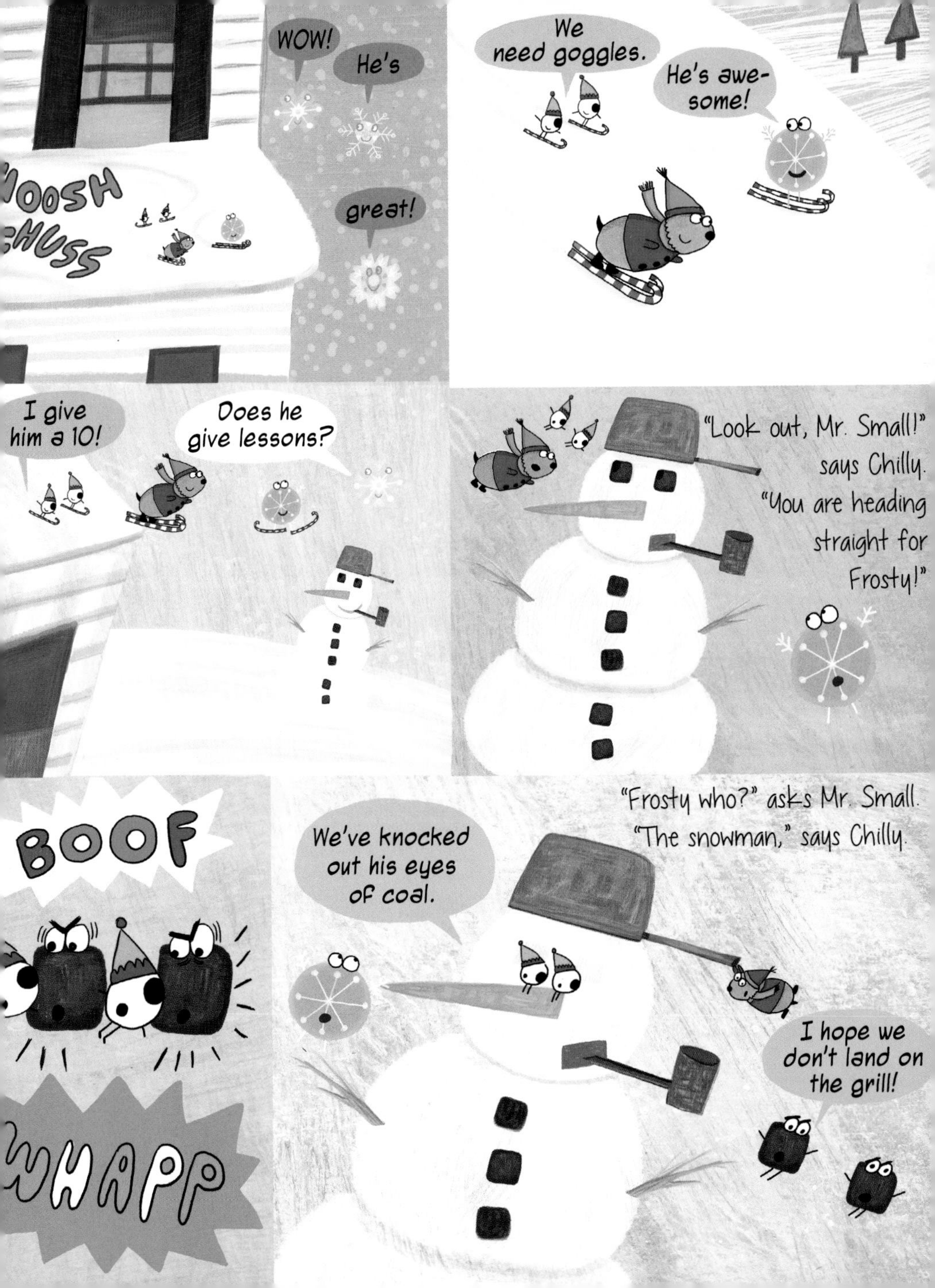
OOSH
HUSS
WOW!
He's
great!
We need goggles.
He's awe-some!
I give him a 10!
Does he give lessons?
"Look out, Mr. Small!" says Chilly. "You are heading straight for Frosty!"
BOOF
WHAPP
"Frosty who?" asks Mr. Small. "The snowman," says Chilly.
We've knocked out his eyes of coal.
I hope we don't land on the grill!

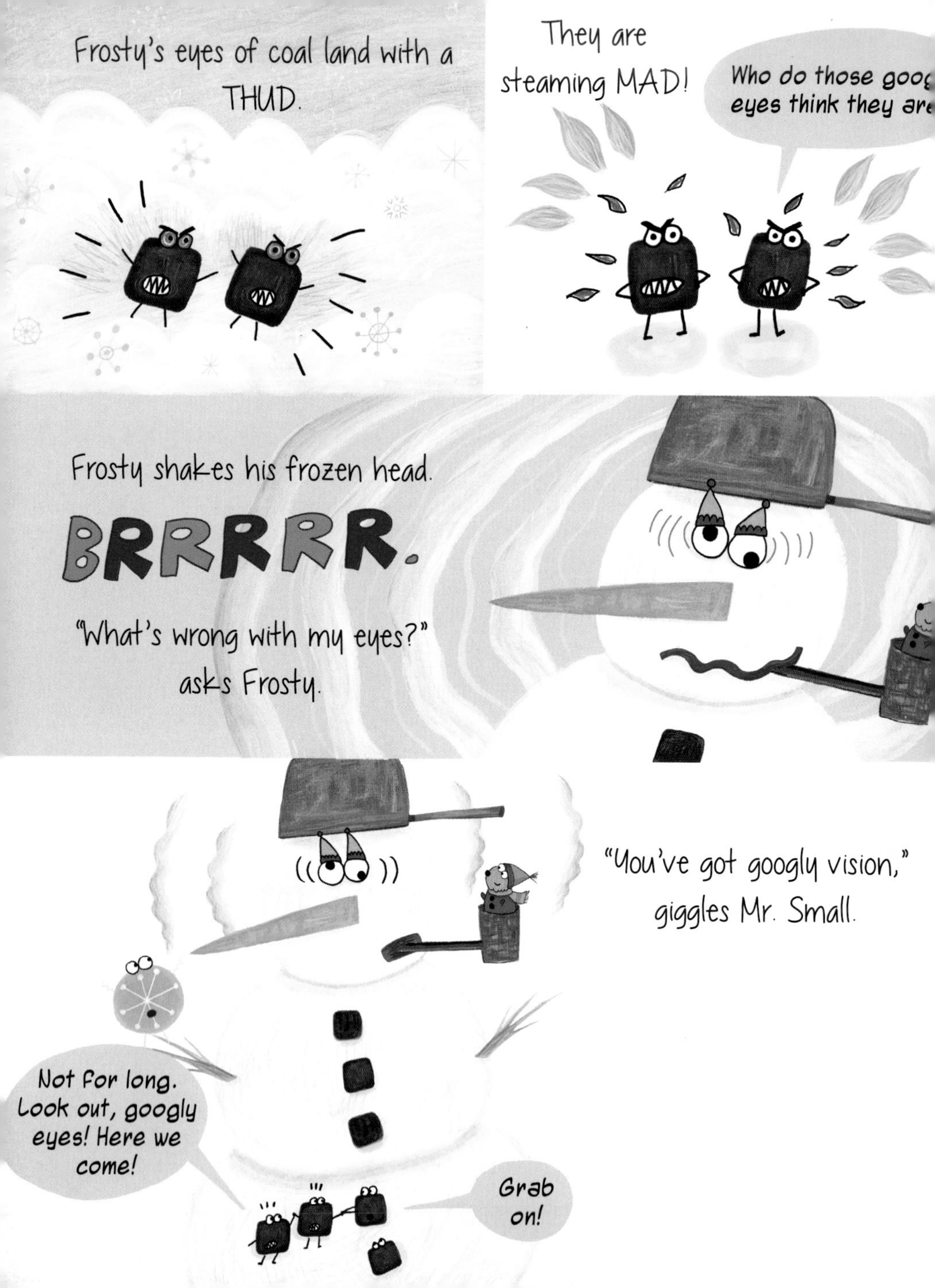
Frosty's eyes of coal land with a THUD.
They are steaming MAD!
Who do those goog
eyes think they ar
Frosty shakes his frozen head.
BRRRRR.
"What's wrong with my eyes?" asks Frosty.
"You've got googly vision," giggles Mr. Small.
Not for long. Look out, googly eyes! Here we come!
Grab on!

"What in all the blurry, freezing world are you?" wonders Frosty.

"I am a hamster," says Mr. Small.

"Who made you?" asks Frosty.

"I don't know," says Mr. Small. "Who made you?"

"The kids built me out of snow," boasts Frosty. "And they gave me a corn cob pipe and a carrot nose and two eyes made out of coal."
"No button for a nose?" asks Chilly.
"They couldn't find one," explains Frosty.
"Could I make something out of snow, too?" asks Mr. Small.

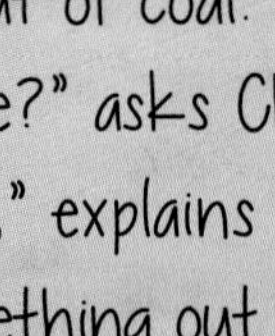

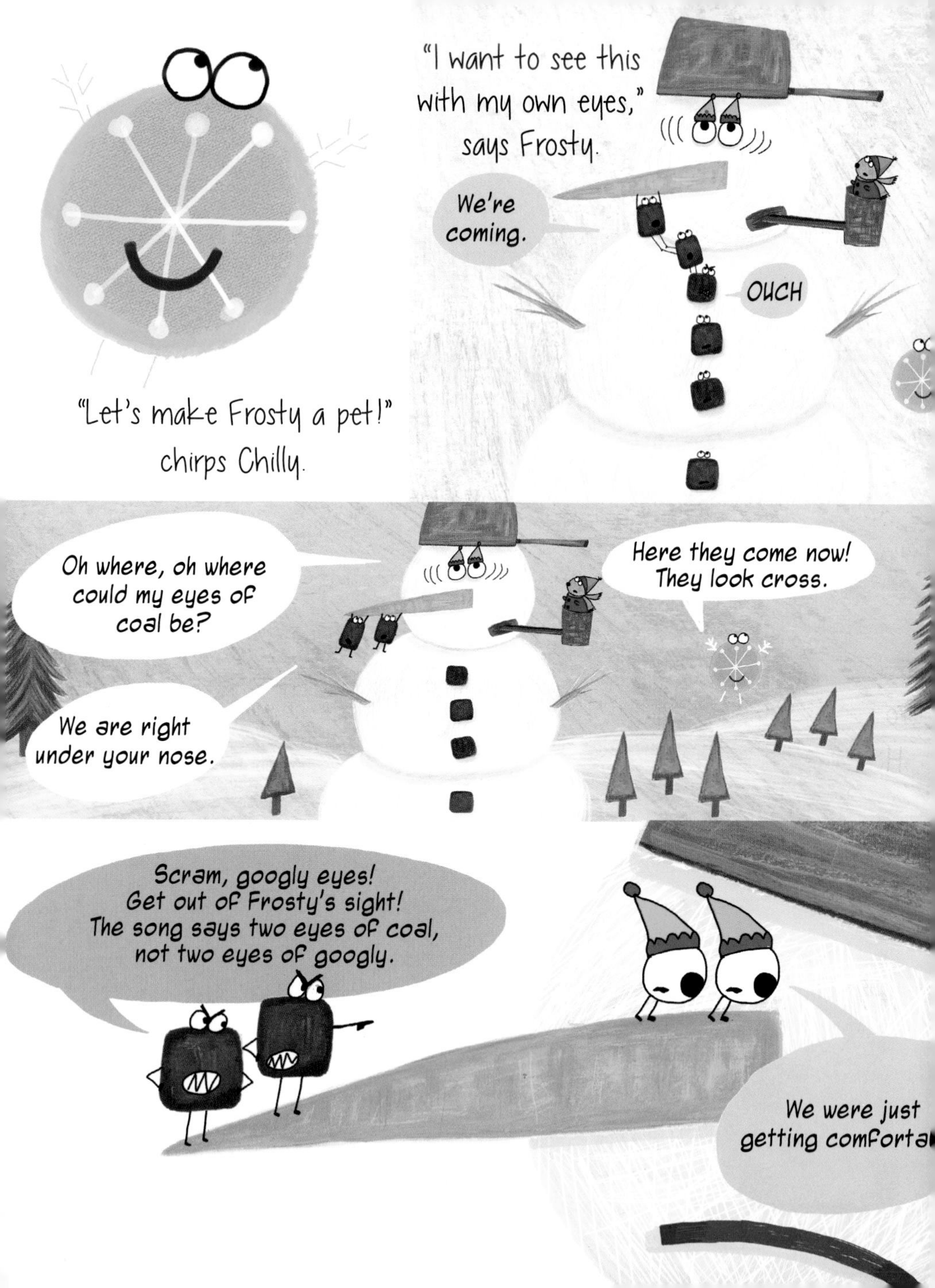
"Let's make Frosty a pet!" chirps Chilly.
"I want to see this with my own eyes," says Frosty.
We're coming.
OUCH
Oh where, oh where could my eyes of coal be?
We are right under your nose.
Here they come now! They look cross.
Scram, googly eyes! Get out of Frosty's sight! The song says two eyes of coal, not two eyes of googly.
We were just getting comforta

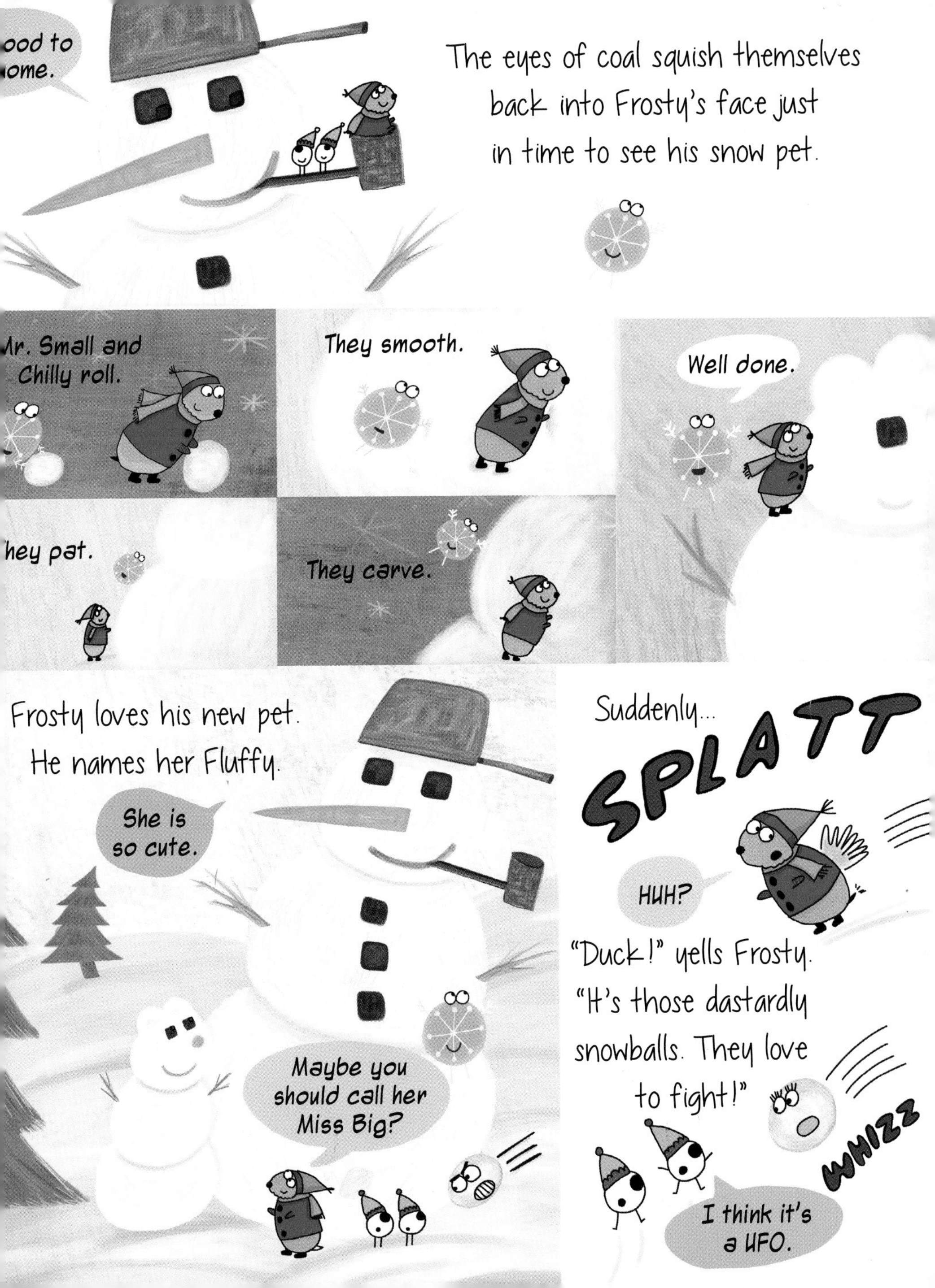
ood to
ome.
The eyes of coal squish themselves back into Frosty's face just in time to see his snow pet.
r. Small and Chilly roll.
They smooth.
Well done.
hey pat.
They carve.
Frosty loves his new pet. He names her Fluffy.
She is so cute.
Maybe you should call her Miss Big?
Suddenly...
SPLATT
HUH?
"Duck!" yells Frosty. "It's those dastardly snowballs. They love to fight!"
WHIZZ
I think it's a UFO.

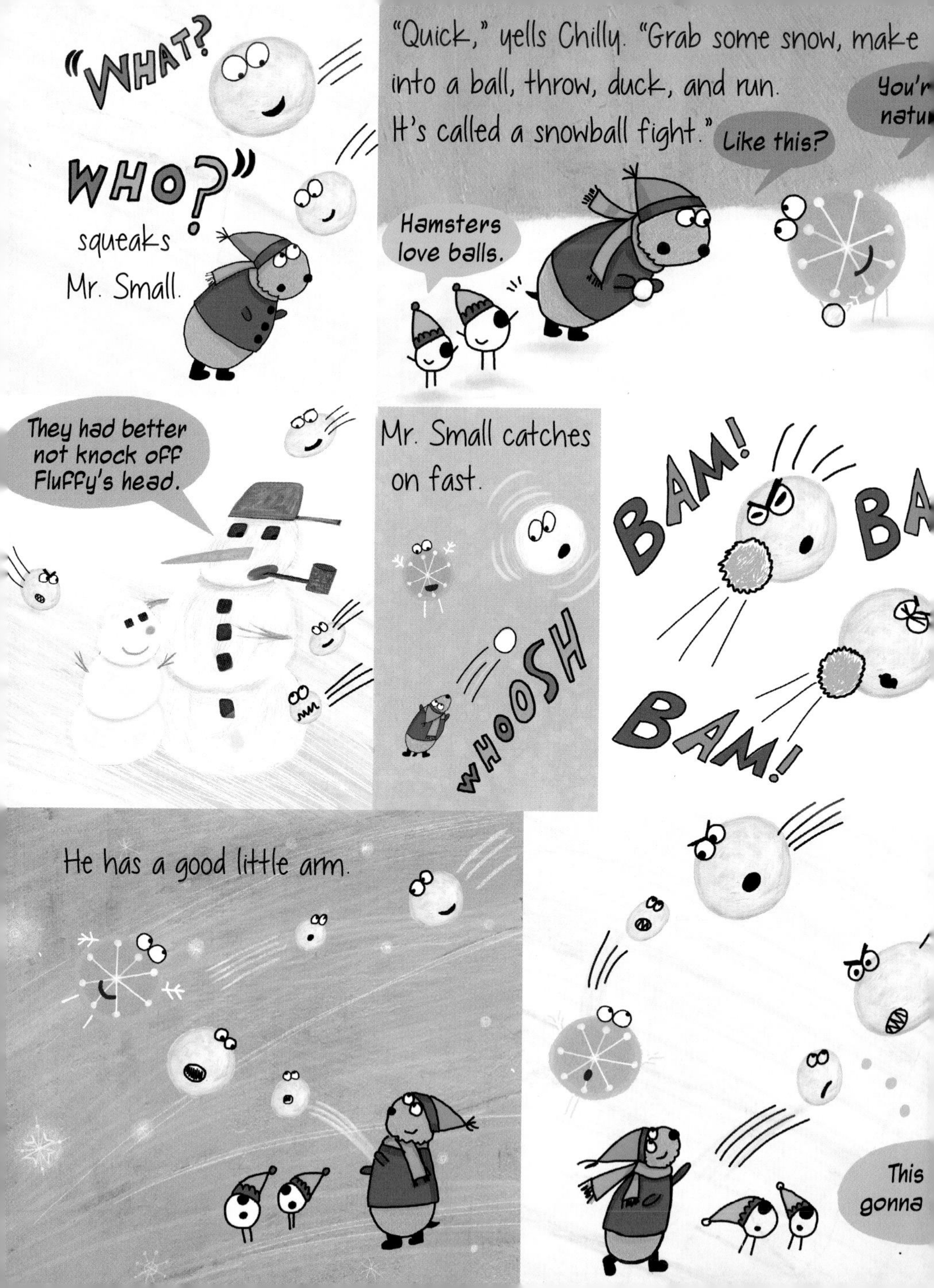
"WHAT?
WHO?"
squeaks Mr. Small.
"Quick," yells Chilly. "Grab some snow, make into a ball, throw, duck, and run. It's called a snowball fight."
Like this?
Hamsters love balls.
They had better not knock off Fluffy's head.
Mr. Small catches on fast.
WHOOSH
BAM!
BAM!
He has a good little arm.

re comes a BIG one!

Rolling! Rolling! Rolling!

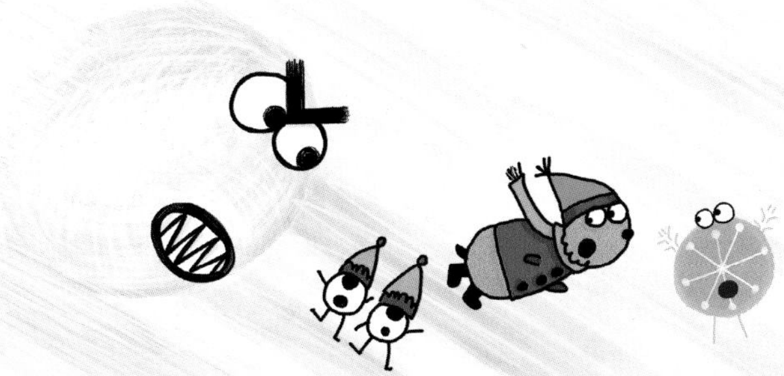

It gobbles up Mr. Small and Chilly.

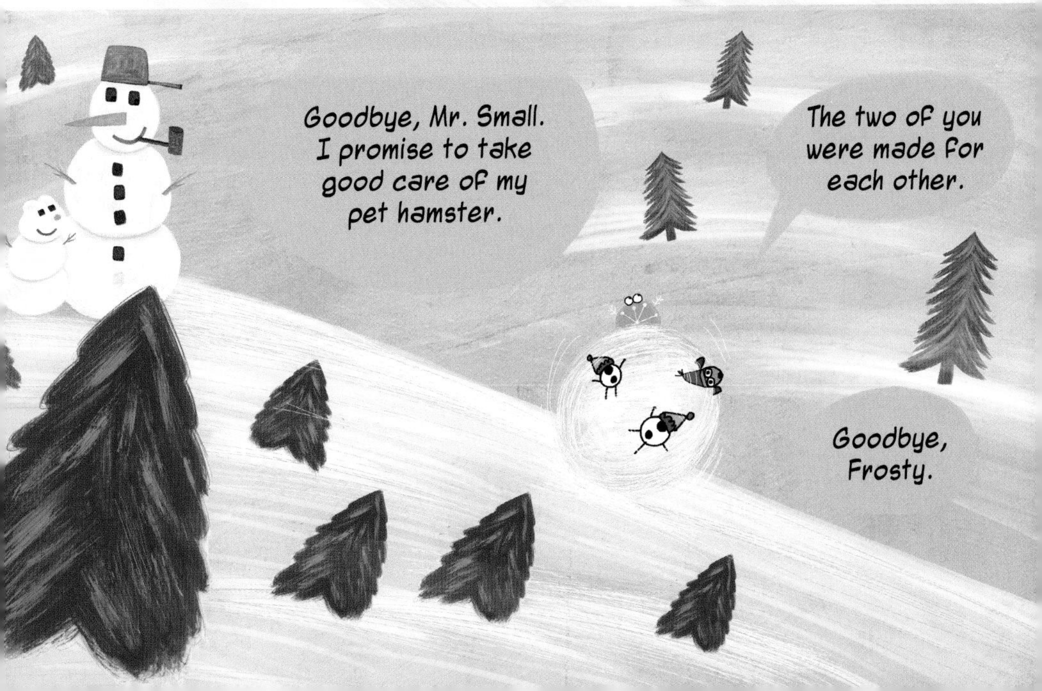
Goodbye, Mr. Small. I promise to take good care of my pet hamster.
The two of you were made for each other.
Goodbye, Frosty.

O OOF

BAM!

Good thing Mr. Small has some extra furry padding.

They whirl.

It was a puddle. Now it's a pond.

What is this stuff?

They twirl.

It's frozen water, otherwise known as ice. It's hard and slippery.

They spin.

OH NO...

Mr. Small is on thin ice! It is not a good idea for a teeny tiny hamster to go swimming in the freezing water.

Ooops

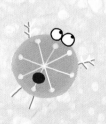

CRACK CRACK

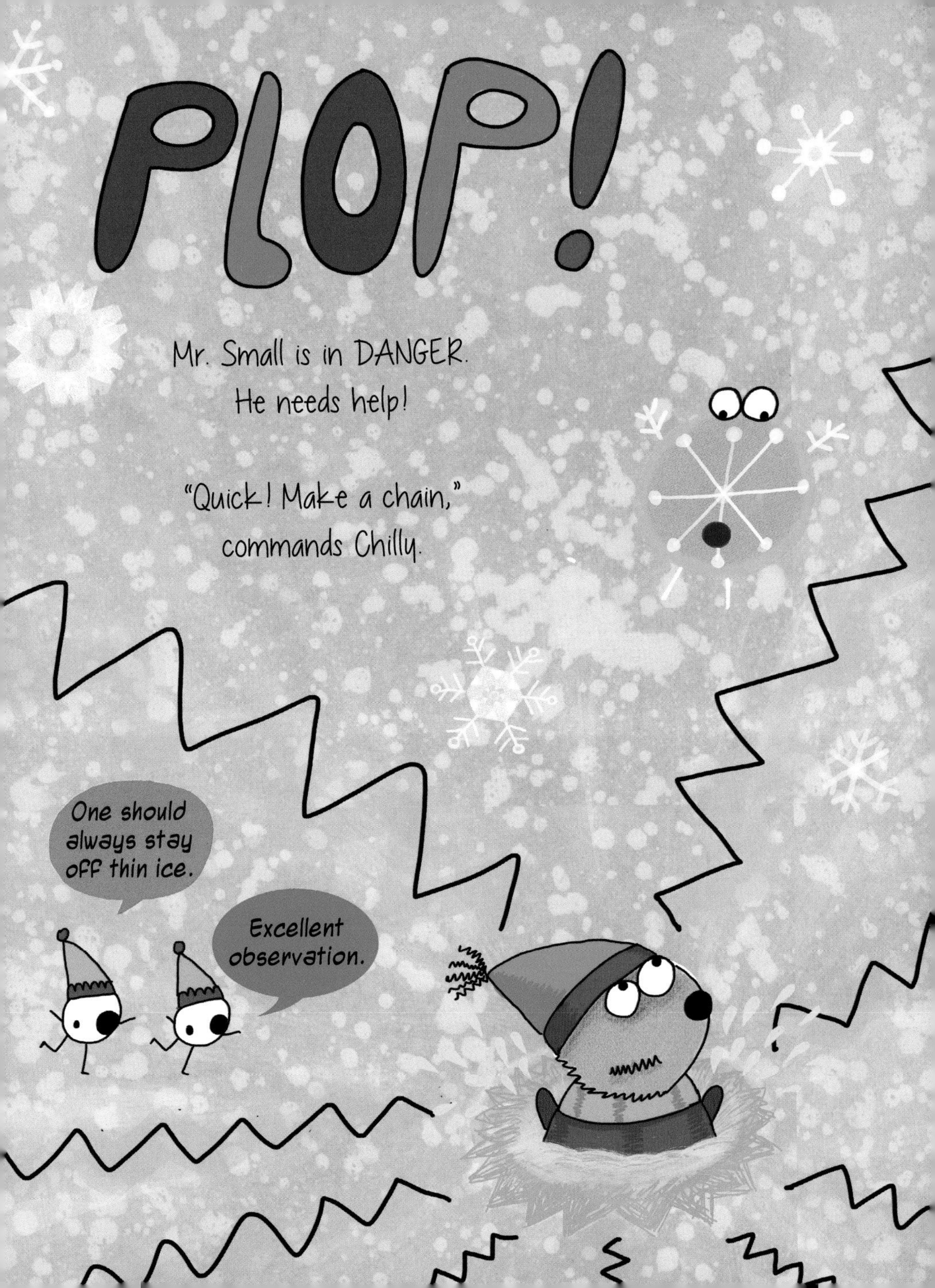
PLOP!
Mr. Small is in DANGER.
He needs help!
"Quick! Make a chain,"
commands Chilly.
One should always stay off thin ice.
Excellent observation.

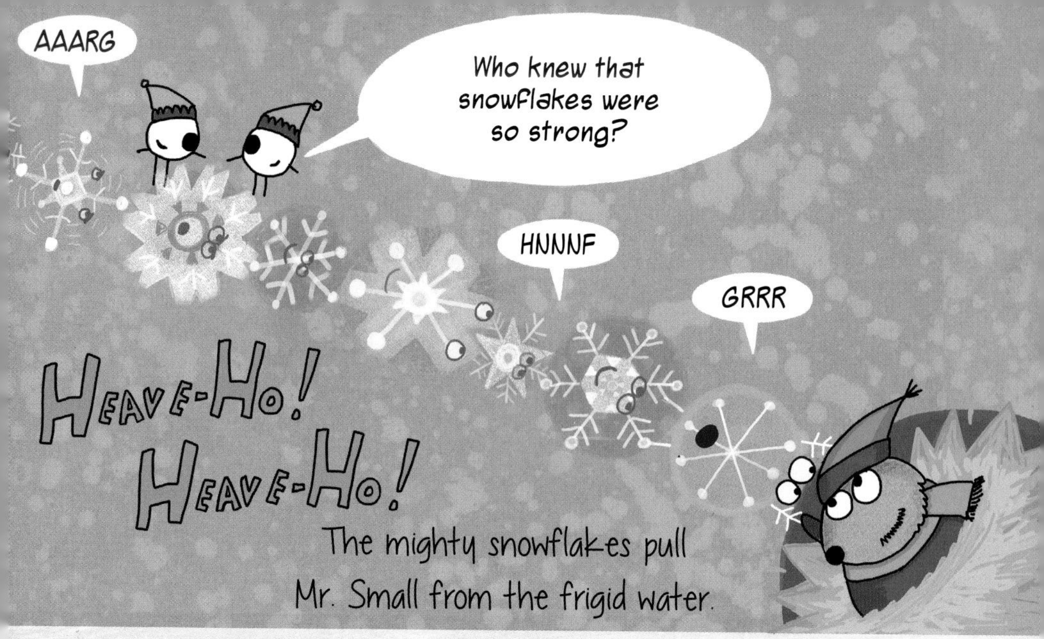
AAARG
Who knew that snowflakes were so strong?
HNNNF
GRRR
HEAVE-HO!
HEAVE-HO!

The mighty snowflakes pull Mr. Small from the frigid water.

Is this the end of our frozen friend, Mr. Small?

"HOWL, COME QUICKLY!" calls Chilly.

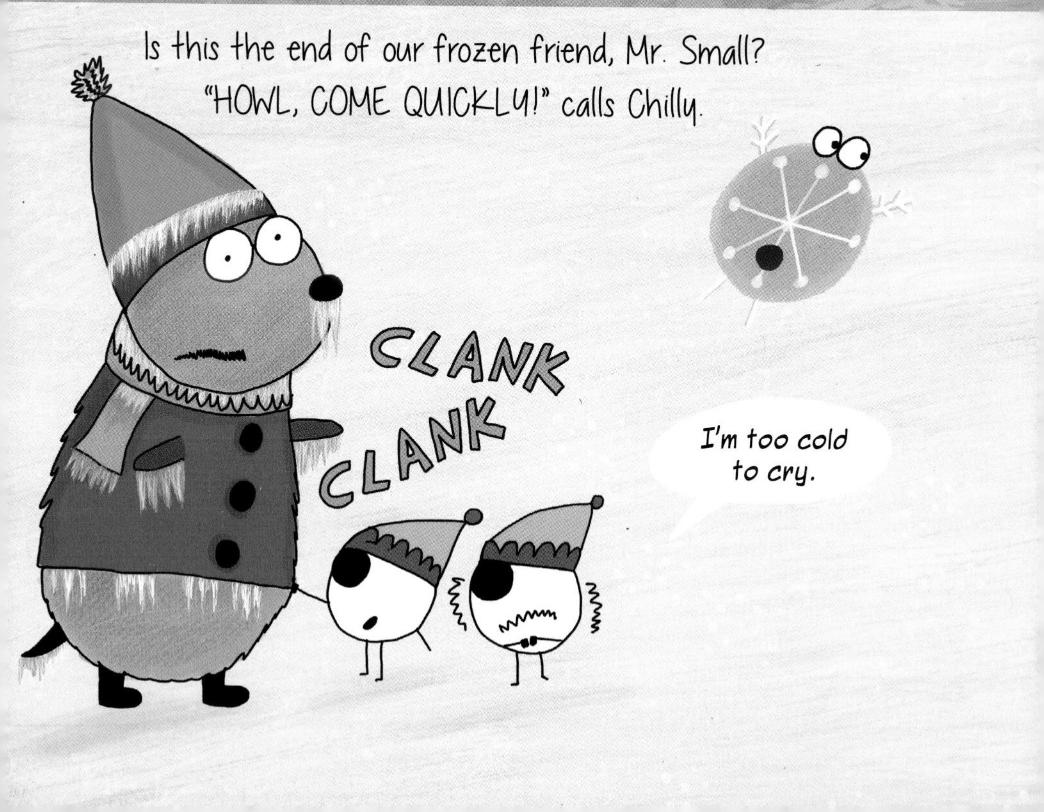
CLANK
CLANK
I'm too cold to cry.

A gust of wind tears through the crisp air.

"What do we have here?" asks Howl.

"A frozen hamster!" Chilly cries.

"We need to get him to Spark, fast!"

Howl puffs with all her might. The trees shake.

The snowflakes swirl.

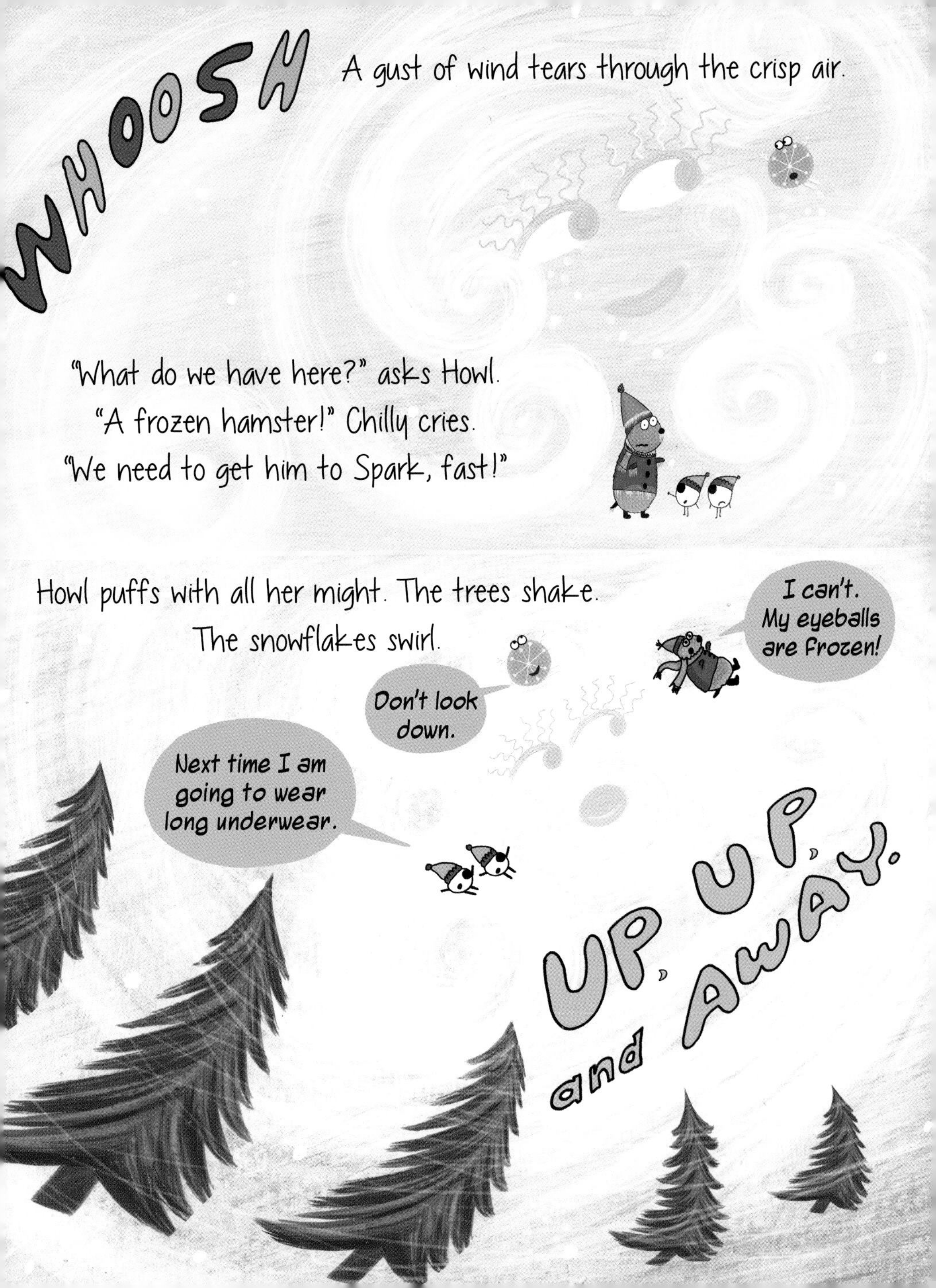
WHOOSH
I can't. My eyeballs are frozen!
Don't look down.
Next time I am going to wear long underwear.
UP, UP, and AWAY.

"I've got another cold one for you, Spark," blows Howl.
"Don't put him too close," crackles Spark,
"I don't want to cook him."

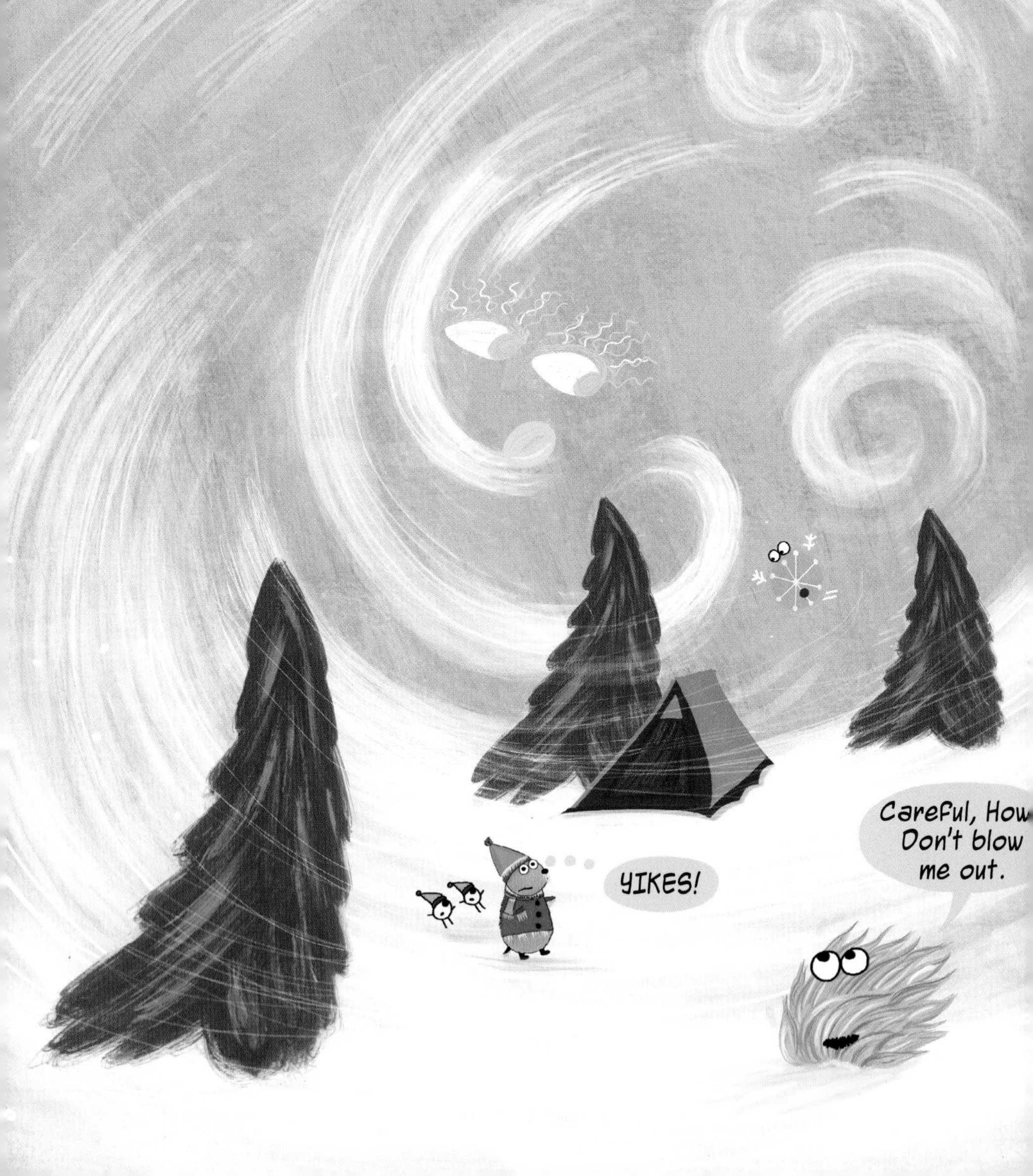
YIKES!
Careful, How Don't blow me out.

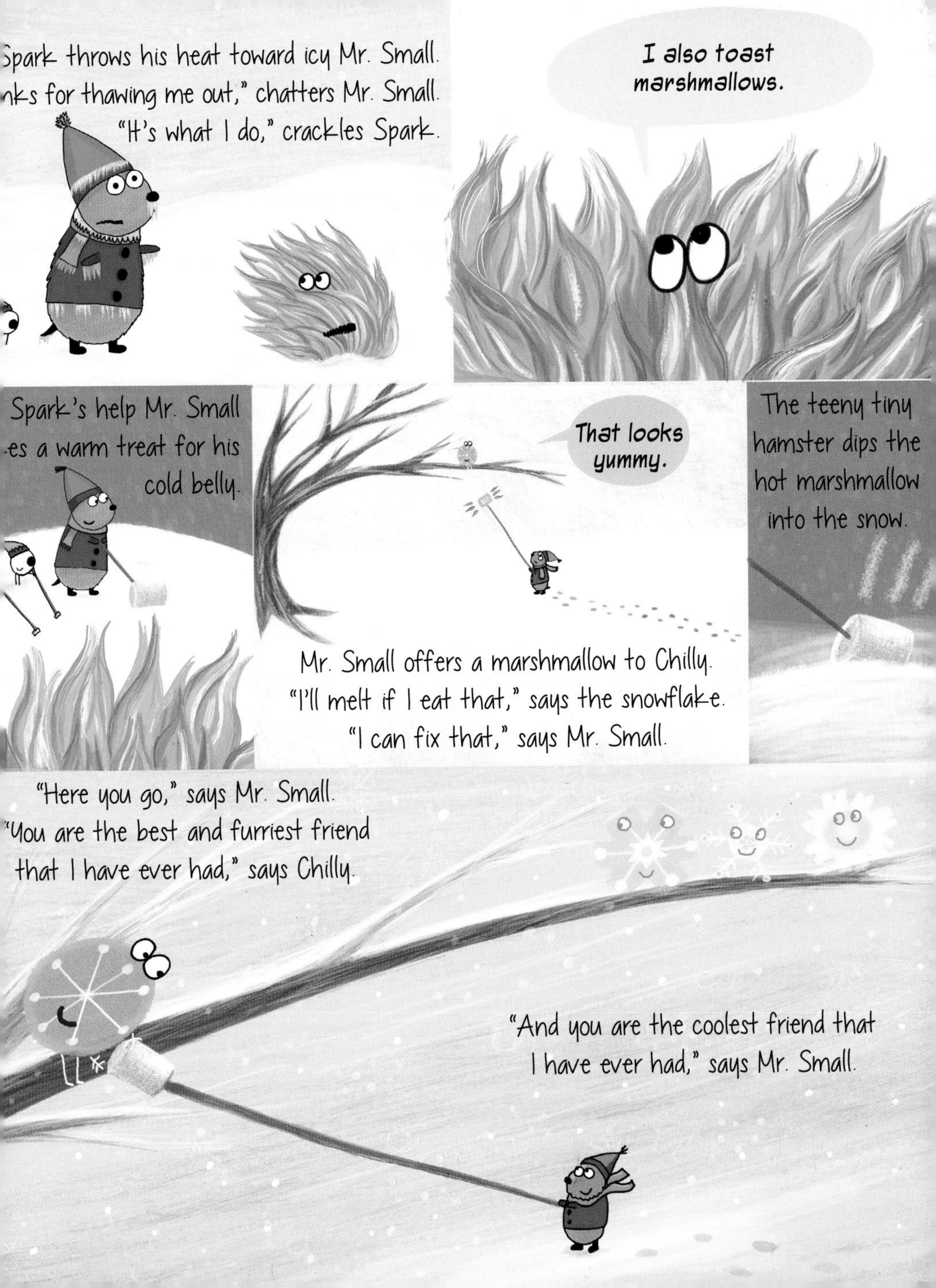
Spark throws his heat toward icy Mr. Small.
nks for thawing me out," chatters Mr. Small.
"It's what I do," crackles Spark.
I also toast marshmallows.
Spark's help Mr. Small
es a warm treat for his
cold belly.
That looks yummy.
The teeny tiny hamster dips the hot marshmallow into the snow.
Mr. Small offers a marshmallow to Chilly.
"I'll melt if I eat that," says the snowflake.
"I can fix that," says Mr. Small.
"Here you go," says Mr. Small.
"You are the best and furriest friend
that I have ever had," says Chilly.
"And you are the coolest friend that
I have ever had," says Mr. Small.

Spark dims. Mr. Small's teeth chatter. "I sure wish you didn't freeze so easily," says Chilly.

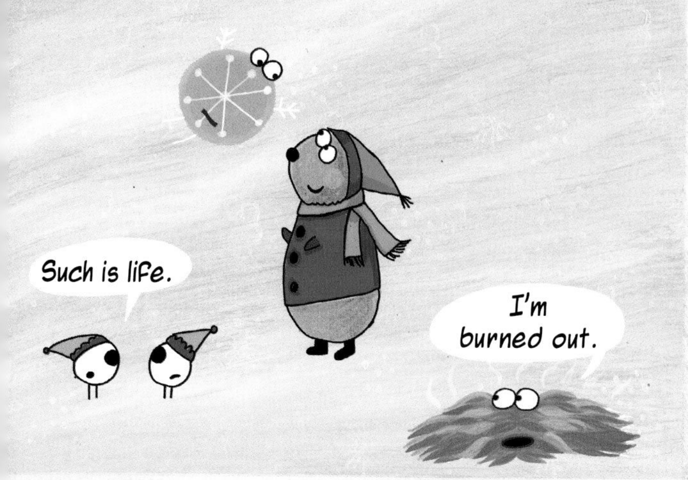
Such is life.
I'm burned out.

It is time for our brav
little hamster to go hom

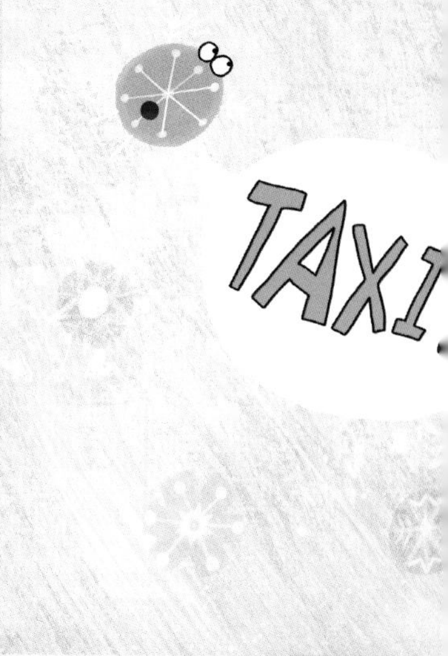
TAXI

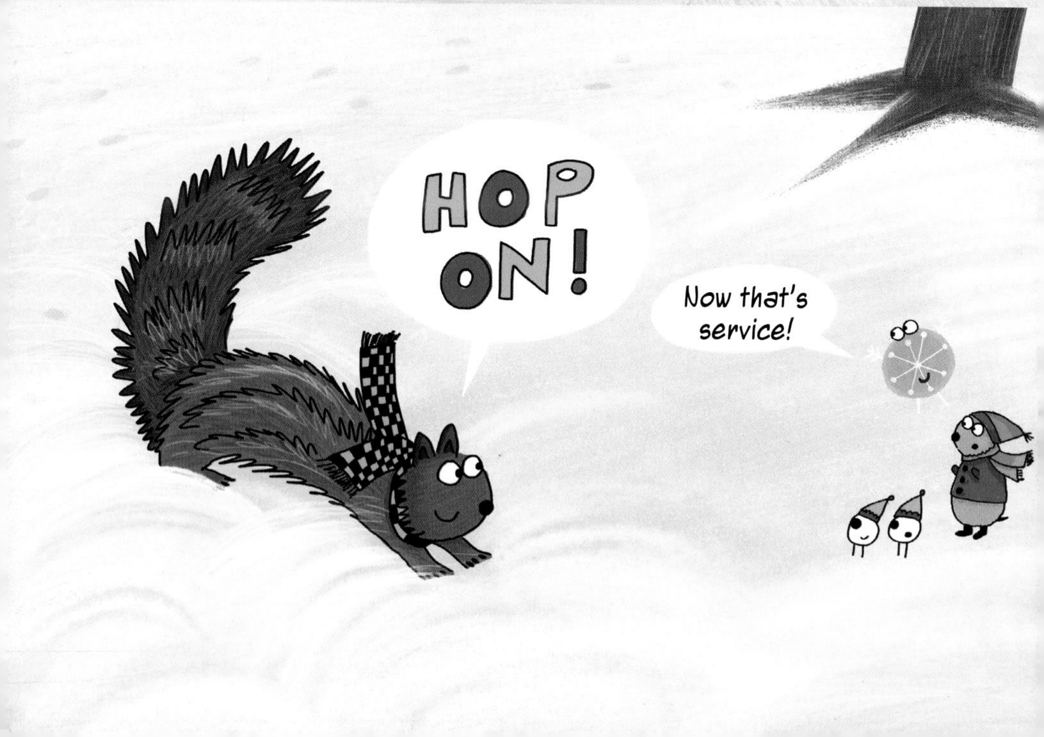
HOP ON!
Now that's service!

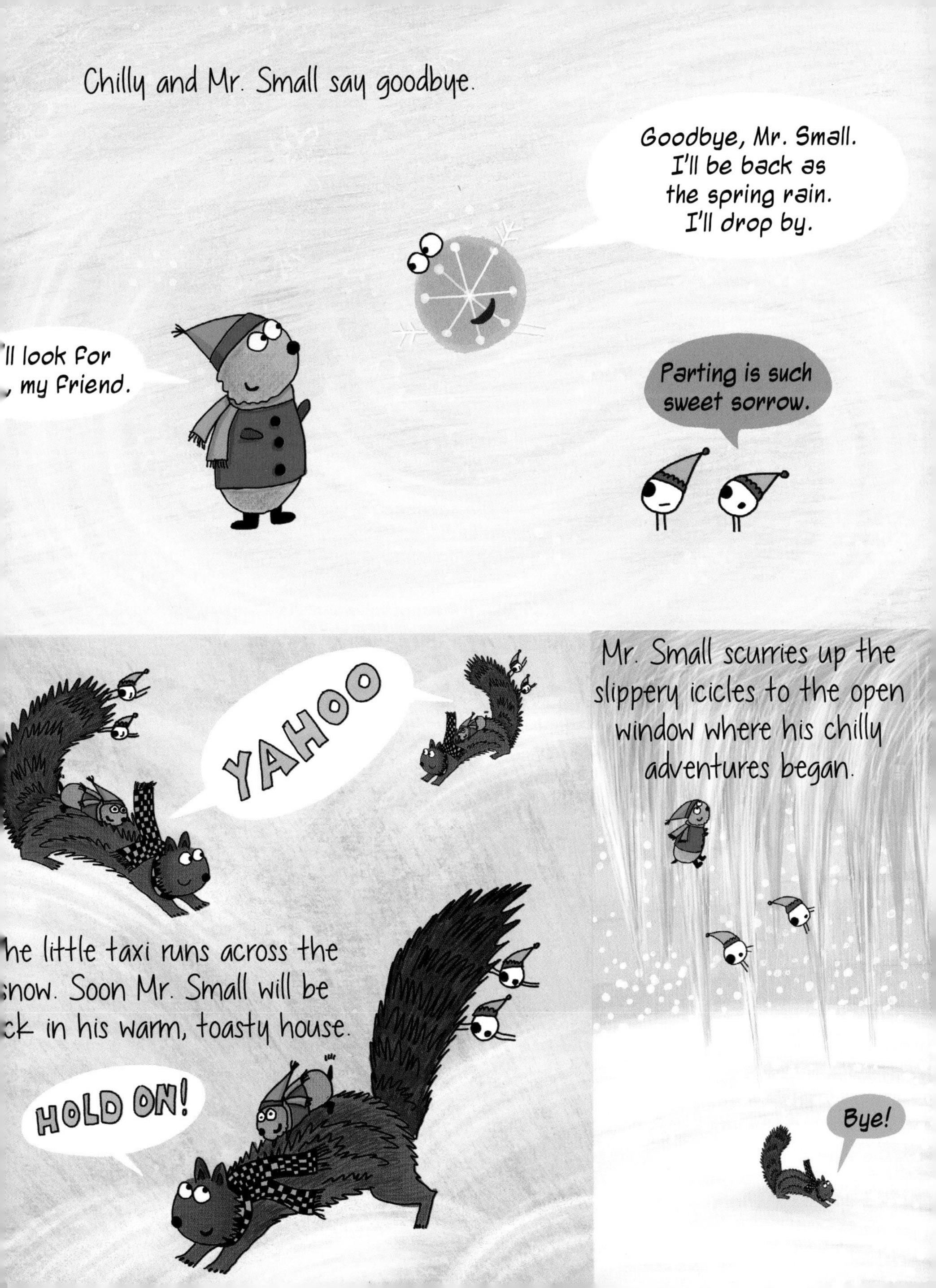
Chilly and Mr. Small say goodbye.
Goodbye, Mr. Small. I'll be back as the spring rain. I'll drop by.
'll look for , my friend.
Parting is such sweet sorrow.
YAHOO
he little taxi runs across the now. Soon Mr. Small will be ck in his warm, toasty house.
HOLD ON!
Mr. Small scurries up the slippery icicles to the open window where his chilly adventures began.
Bye!

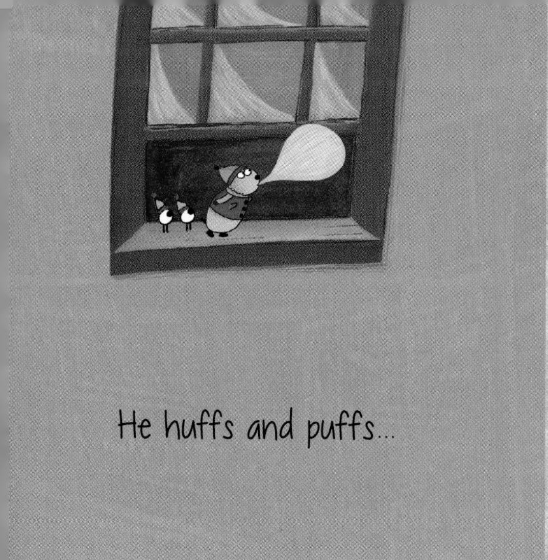
He huffs and puffs...

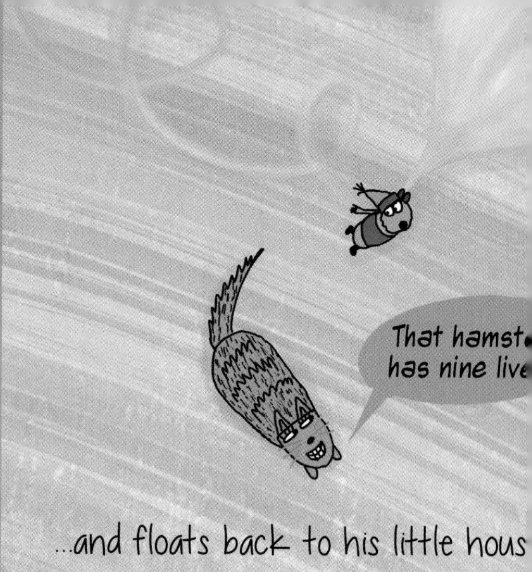
That hamst
has nine live
...and floats back to his little hous

Teeny tiny hamsters love big adventures, but it is always good to be back home safe and sound with a good friend and a steaming cup of cocoa.

"Thanks, Dusty," squeaks Mr. Small.

"You are welcome, Mr. Small," says Big Dusty.

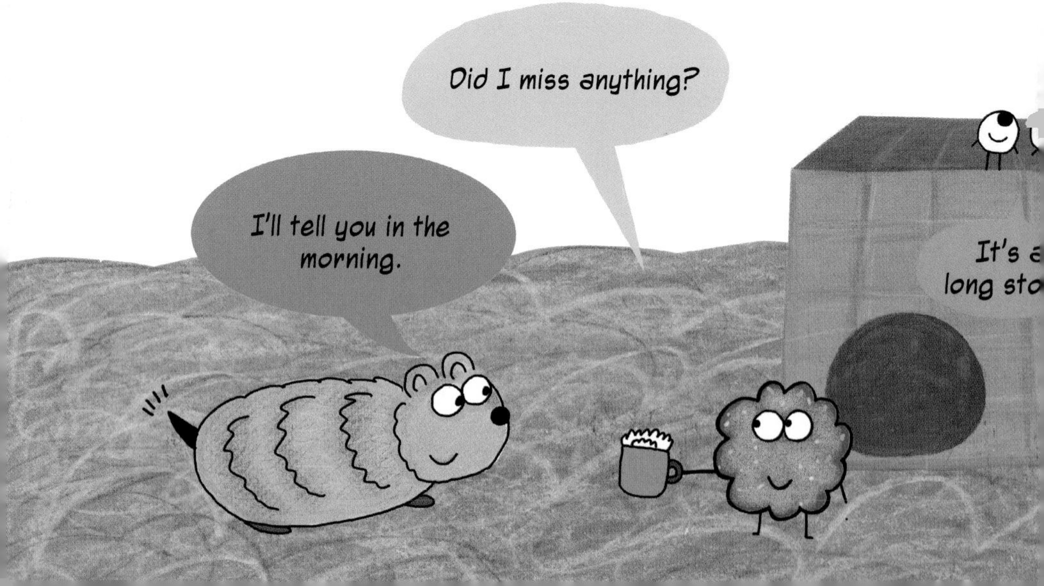
Did I miss anything?
I'll tell you in the morning.
It's a
long sto

Mr. Small tucks Big Dusty in and buries himself in an extra layer of fluff.

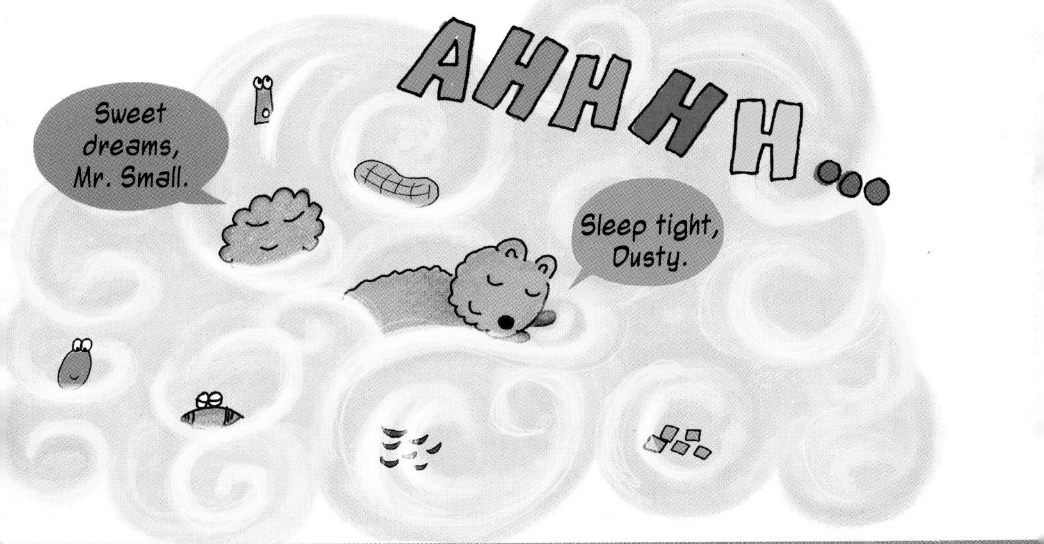

Sweet dreams, Mr. Small.
AHHHH...
Sleep tight, Dusty.


Mr. Small wakes with a start. He still has one more adventure left.

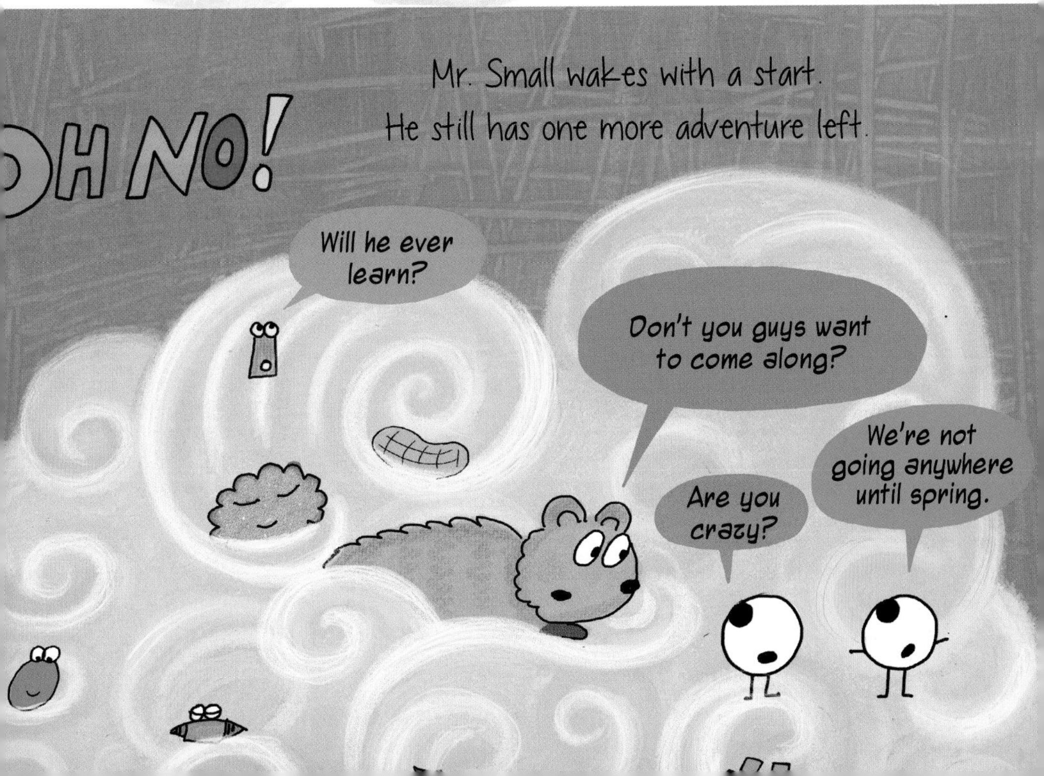

OH NO!
Will he ever learn?
Don't you guys want to come along?
Are you crazy?
We're not going anywhere until spring.

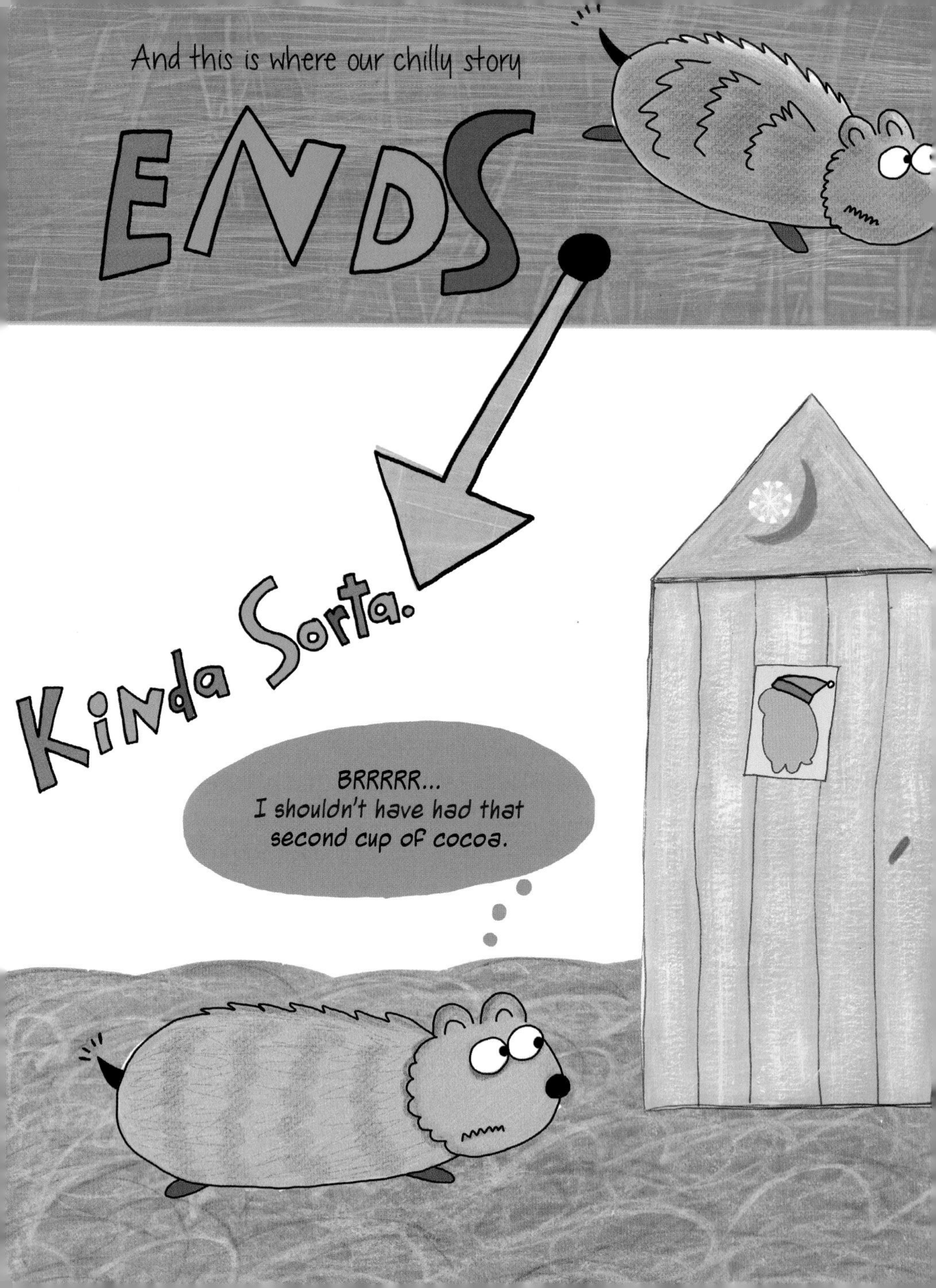
And this is where our chilly story
ENDS.
Kinda Sorta.
BRRRRR...
I shouldn't have had that
second cup of cocoa.